Heart

by

Graysen Morgen

2012

Secluded Heart © 2012 Graysen Morgen
Triplicity Publishing, LLC

ISBN-13: 978-1477410677
ISBN-10: 1477410678

All rights reserved. No part of this publication may be reproduced, distributed, or transmitted in any form without permission.

This is a work of fiction. Names, characters, places, and incidents are the product of the author's imagination and are used fictitiously. Any resemblance to actual persons, living or dead, business establishments, events, or locales is entirely coincidental.

Printed in the United States of America
First Edition – 2012
Revised - 2024
Cover Design: Triplicity Publishing, LLC
Interior Design: Triplicity Publishing, LLC

Also by Graysen Morgen

Falling Snow

Fate vs. Destiny

Just Me

Love Loss Revenge

Natural Instinct

Submerged

To my loving wife, you make it possible for me to write these stories. Thank you for everything you do.

Chapter 1

The silver convertible Mercedes roadster parallel parked by the curb. When the door opened, a woman with short, messy blond hair stepped out. She was dressed in a black business suit with a light pink blouse underneath. As soon as she walked through the doors of Rainer's, a local coffee house with a soup and sandwich deli, she heard the familiar voices and made her way to their usual table.

"It's about time you made it, we were going to order without you." The auburn-haired woman sitting at the table flashed a smile. She was dressed business casual in a crème-colored sleeveless top and khaki pants.

"Frankie, I'm not in the mood for it. So, I'm late, big deal." The blond sat down and took a sip from the water glass in front of her. She was already sweating from the blistering Miami heat in the middle of March and was sure her business suit would be soaked before the day was over.

"Ouch! What crawled up your butt, Chase?" Another woman sitting at the table asked. She had short spiky jet-black hair and was dressed in chinos and a polo shirt.

"Nothing," the blond barked.

"French bitch?" The last person to join the table, a tiny Asian woman in a charcoal gray skirt suit, butted into the conversation as she sat down.

"Would you stop calling her that?" Chase snapped. She really couldn't stay mad at her best friends, even though they called her girlfriend 'French bitch'. She had to laugh. Yes, her girlfriend was French, and she could definitely be a bitch at times.

"Okay, how about playboy bunny?"

"Look, we had a fight this morning. Cut me some slack."

"Chase, we're only razing you, we like Yelena," Frankie said.

"How about a subject change?"

"Good idea, Ping Pong."

Chase looked around the table. Frankie, short for Francis, was the oldest at thirty-six, but didn't look a day over thirty. Her auburn hair hung loose around her shoulders and her hazel eyes stood out gracefully. She was taller than Chase, especially in the heels she usually wore. Frankie owned and operated her own art gallery in South Beach, where many major artists were shown each month. The ebony haired woman sitting next to Frankie was Gayle Vincent, a thirty-one-year-old computer programmer. Chase had dated her for a month a few years ago and realized they were better off as friends. The last woman at the table was Ping, a five-foot-two inch, thirty-three-year-old Asian woman who looked like she was still eighteen. Ping was an editor for a large fashion magazine.

Chase was the baby of the group, at thirty. She was five-foot-five, so at least she wasn't the shortest, but she definitely didn't look a day over twenty-five. Her short blond hair was kept very short and always worn in the 'I just got out of bed' messy look. Her jade green eyes had a light blue hue around them, sort of like a cat's. Chase was a resident cardiac surgeon at Mount Sinai Hospital. She'd worked very long and very hard to get to where she was at such a young age. All the doctors and surgeons at the hospital looked at her with respect and, of course, the occasional wandering eye.

"So, what's for lunch, ladies?" the salt and pepper haired man asked as he pulled up a chair. A thin pencil was still stuck behind his ear. Paul Rainer, the owner of the place, had known the girls for years. He treated them like family, in a way they *were*, 'gay family' that is. As Chase began to answer him her cell phone rang in her pocket. She reached into her jacket to check the caller ID and decided against answering it. One fight per day with her girlfriend was all that she allowed.

***

"Dr. Leery, please dial one-four-two." The page rang over the hospital loudspeaker. Chase was on her way to the lounge to get a cup of muddy coffee. She grabbed the phone attached to the wall as soon as she walked through the double doors. Her bright blond hair stuck out in contrast to her dark blue scrubs.

"This is Dr. Chase Leery," she said when the woman answered.

"I couldn't find your pager number. I think I have a Mitral Valve Regurgitation," the ER doctor explained.

"Have you ordered an echocardiogram?" she asked.

"Yes, I just got the results, but they aren't back yet."

"I'm on the way." She put the phone down and headed towards the nearest elevator. Her black sneakers squeaked on the freshly waxed floor. As soon as she arrived, she saw the results of the echocardiogram and the ECG.

"Mrs. Neilson, this is Dr. Leery. She's a cardiac surgeon. She's going to talk to you and your family about your test results." The ER attending left the area and pulled the curtain closed.

"I've reviewed all your tests. Unfortunately, I do have bad news for you. Mrs. Neilson, you have Severe Mitral Valve Regurgitation. Your left ventricle is dilated causing displacement of the papillary muscles. You're going to need a mitral valve replacement immediately." She took a deep breath and answered all the family's questions as the woman was wheeled up to the OR.

***

As soon as the surgery was completed, Chase went straight to the woman's family in the waiting area. Her husband and daughter were hunched together in a corner staring at the TV.

"Mr. Neilson, we're finished. She's in stable condition in the recovery room right now. The replacement went well."

"When..." He sniffled. "When can we see her?"

"As soon as she's out of recovery and moved to cardiac intensive care for further monitoring. She'll be asleep for a while. She needs her rest."

"Thank you, doctor."

Chase nodded and squeezed his hand. The easy part was over, now the hard part had begun. The surgery procedures were second nature to her, but the after affects and the waiting game always tormented her. Some patients recovered, some didn't. Carrying that kind of failure rate around was not something she wished on anyone's conscience. But honestly, she was one of the best surgeons in Miami. She had no control over the variables such as age or overall health, seventy-five percent of the heart patients were already at risk to begin with. She stopped letting herself *feel* for the patients a long time ago. Chase stood and walked out of the waiting room. She hoped Mrs. Neilson was awake and recovering when she returned in the morning. For now, she was headed back to her tiny office on the cardiac floor to finish some patient charts. She was already twenty hours into overtime for the week. This eight-hour surgery had just added to it.

***

"Hey, I'm home," Chase called out as she walked into the large beachfront condo. Driving a hundred-thousand-dollar car and living in a million-dollar condo was simply property to her, but she did enjoy the lifestyle.

"There you are. I thought you'd be home hours ago. We're meeting your friends at some little bar in town in an hour," Yelena Guichard, a French American model with long, bleach blond hair, big boobs, and fake-tanned skin was the classic style 'playboy bunny.' She was thirty and going through a mid-life crisis. She blew as much of Chase's money as she could every chance she got. Chase's friends hated her, but Chase supposedly loved the woman, so they tolerated her air-headedness.

"I had emergency surgery to tend to," Chase said as she stripped out of her scrubs and headed towards the shower.

***

"Here they come, ladies. Everyone behave," Frankie said when saw Chase enter the bar with Yelena at her side.

"I still don't know what she sees in that bitch," Ping added.

"Ssshh!" Frankie hissed. "Hey, Chase." She leaned in and gave her friend a hug. "Hi, Yelena." Chase hugged all her friends then turned towards the bar to order a drink. After the day she'd had, she was looking forward to a stiff cocktail. The band was just about to take the stage.

"Have you ever heard these girls play?" Yelena asked sarcastically.

"Of course we have, they're awesome," Gayle retorted and rolled her eyes.

The blues band began playing a familiar cover song. Women and men were dancing and drinking, having a good time. Yelena was appalled at what she saw. She expected them to be at some ritzy salsa club throwing around money with the high rollers of the city.

"I'm ready to go," she said loud enough for the group to hear her.

"Right now? The band just started."

"Yes, Chase. Right now," she huffed and began to storm out of the tiny bar. She turned around with her hands on her hips to make sure she was being followed.

"I need to go. I'll call you." Chase rolled her eyes and walked out of the bar.

Chapter 2

Chase changed from her scrubs into a black pantsuit and a baby-blue blouse and hurried towards the hospital parking garage. The physician parking was on the third level, so she took the elevator.

Minutes later, Chase was parking the Mercedes roadster in downtown South Beach. She got out and walked into the Deluca Art Gallery.

"Good afternoon, Dr. Leery. Ms. Deluca is expecting you." Chase walked into the large office at the end of the hallway as Frankie was hanging up the phone.

"Hey!"

"Sorry I'm late. I had a cardio angioplasty run longer than expected," Chase said as she collapsed into the leather chair in front of the large wooden desk. Various paintings covered the surrounding walls.

"You look beat. Are you still working a hundred hours a week?"

"Yeah." She closed her eyes and yawned.

"Chase you're going to kill yourself working like that. What the hell's going on with that hospital?"

"Honestly, it's not a staffing problem." She

stretched; her leg muscles were still sore from her morning jog. She had run the five miles half asleep as usual. "I've just had a lot of consultations on top of surgeries every day. And there's also emergencies that must be dealt with every day. Those push everything back. I've had six emergencies in the past three days."

"Goodness, no wonder you're tired. How are things at home?"

Chase rolled her eyes. "Fine."

"You can't lie to me." The auburn-haired woman took on a serious tone. "I've told you from the beginning that I'm not going to butt in. I just don't understand why you let her run all over you and spend your money like it grows on trees."

"It's only money, Frankie."

"Yeah, well it's not hers to spend," she huffed. "She treats you like shit and you let her."

"I didn't come here to argue with you about Yelena."

"Good. I don't care to talk about her anyway."

"Do you have anything good coming in?" Chase asked, changing the subject.

"Yeah, I have a few new artists that I've been meeting with. I'm trying to put a show together for next month."

"That gives me something to look forward to." Chase smiled. "I need to run. I have a meeting at the Heart Institute at two o'clock. I'm supposed to give a seminar there next week." Chase stood up and walked towards the door.

"Call me later if you wanna go have a drink. I should be out of here about six."

Chase closed the office door and walked into the

Secluded Heart

lobby area of the gallery. She immediately noticed the woman sitting in a chair close to the secretary's desk. She had short, brown hair that was cut identical to Chase's and big brown eyes. Her olive complexion blended in perfectly with her black pantsuit and white blouse. *She's cute.* Chase smiled, stopped in front of the woman, and stuck her hand out. "Hi, I'm Chase..." Before she could finish her sentence Frankie's secretary came running down the hall towards her.

"Dr. Leery, you left your keys on Ms. Deluca's desk." The bubbly blond handed Chase her car keys.

"Thanks." Chase turned back towards the woman in the chair and offered her hand again. "Sorry, *Doctor* Chase Leery." When the woman's soft hand touched her own, she literally felt her heart skip a beat. *Get control of yourself, Leery!*

"I'm Remy Sheridan. It's nice to meet you." She smiled, still holding the hand that was offered to her. Seconds passed before she let go.

Chase smiled once again as she left the building.

***

Two weeks later, Chase was sitting in Rainer's on Sunday afternoon with Gayle, Frankie, and Ping. Luckily for the group of friends, Yelena was out of town on a photo shoot. Chase was wearing thin tan pants that resembled scrubs, a white tank top and flip flops. All the women were dressed causal and comfortable, sitting around drinking coffee and eating blueberry crepes.

"So, I hear you picked up a new artist, Frankie," Ping said between bites of crepe.

"Yeah, she's going to be shown in a couple of

weeks."

"What does she look like?"

"Gayle, do you always have to be so pigheaded?" Chase cut in with sarcasm.

"She's young, cute, and straight. She has a boyfriend."

"That's never stopped Gayle," Ping laughed.

"What's her style?" Chase sipped her coffee.

"She's very abstract, lots of color. Actually, you'd probably like it."

"Yeah, but it won't go with your Monet's," Gayle snickered.

Chase lost all train of thought when the front door opened and Remy Sheridan walked in wearing jeans, a black tank top and flip flops. She went right to the counter to place her order. Chase was starring in that direction and Frankie snapped her fingers in front of Chase's nose to get her attention.

"What!" She barked at her friend.

"That's my new artist," Frankie laughed. "The one you're gazing at with your tongue hanging out."

"I was not!" Chase shook her head. "I met her at your office a couple weeks ago."

"You did?"

"Yeah, she was waiting to meet with you."

"She doesn't look straight, but then again, we don't all look gay either," Gayle laughed.

"Wow, she's definitely easy on the eyes," Ping said with a smile as she checked out the newcomer.

"She's really quiet actually. Did she speak to you in my office?" Frankie asked as she sipped her coffee.

"Yeah, but only for a second though."

"Hmm..." Frankie could see the look in her best

friend's eyes. Chase was watching every move the woman at the counter made. "Go talk to her."

"Yeah, Chase, go get her." Ping egged her on.

Chase couldn't hide the smile when she rolled her eyes and stood up. "I need another cup of coffee anyway." She forgot about the waitress that was heading towards the table. Instead, she walked right up to the woman and was surprised to see she was at least three inches taller.

"Hi, Remy." Chase stared into chocolate brown eyes.

"Hi." She smiled shyly. "Dr. Leery, right?"

Chased grinned. "Yeah, please call me Chase."

"What kind of doctor are you?"

Chase placed her order for another cup of hazelnut coffee. "I'm a cardiac surgeon at Mount Sinai."

"Wow."

"Hey, I'm sitting with some friends, would you like to join us?"

"Nah, I'm… I have some errands to run."

"Frankie's with us."

Remy looked confused. "Who?"

"I'm sorry, you know her as Francis Deluca."

"Oh. Well, tell her I said hi. I should get going."

"It was nice to see you again."

Remy smiled and continued to stare into Chase's green eyes, then she turned and left the restaurant. Chase made her way back to the table. Something about that woman sent her libido into high gear.

"So?" Gayle asked, sitting on the edge of her seat.

"What? Oh, she said hi Frankie."

"That's it?"

"Pretty much, she's very shy."

"You should ask her out."

"Gayle, I'm with Yelena. Besides, she has a boyfriend. Didn't you hear Frankie?"

"So."

"She's adorable. I'll admit I'm very attracted to her, but I don't have to act on it. I'm not a single, horny teenager."

"Yeah, yeah,"

"I need to get going. Yelena's plane comes in at noon. If I'm not waiting inside the terminal, she'll flip out." Chase stood up and stretched.

"God forbid French bitch would have to wait on you or carry her own damn luggage outside."

Chase didn't retort, she simply shrugged her shoulders and waved as she left.

***

Chase ran a hand through her short messy hair as she sat in the terminal waiting area. Yelena's plane was due to land in twenty minutes, so she closed her eyes and leaned her head back. Minutes later, she awoke to the vibrating of her cell phone. She recognized the hospital number on the caller ID.

"Chase Leery."

"I hate to interrupt you on your day off, Dr. Leery, but we have a patient who came in with aortic stenosis. He needs an emergency aortic valve replacement and Dr. Samuel is already in another surgery."

"How constricted is the valve?" she asked.

"It's a little more than fifty millimeters."

"Get him prepped. I'm on the way, but I'm coming from the airport." She slammed the phone closed and dialed Yelena's cell.

"Hey, I'm sorry, I'm not going to be able to pick you up. I just got called for an emergency surgery, so I'm headed to the hospital. I'll call you as soon as I'm out. I'll make sure there's a car service to take you home." She closed the phone and stopped at the rental car area on her way out.

***

Chase changed into an extra pair of scrubs and sneakers that she kept in her office. She hurried down to the OR. Dr. Chaffey, her assistant for this operation, was already scrubbing in. She joined him at the sink and began her scrubbing.

"Did you speak to the family?" she asked as the nurse tied her face mask for her.

"Yeah, I didn't make them any promises. The patient's a sixty-year-old chain smoker." he said in a semi deep voice. His reddish-orange colored hair stuck out from the sides of his sterile cap.

"Wonderful." She shook her head, said a tiny prayer, and did the one thing she knew best, cut the man's chest wide open and began repairing the damage.

***

The Mercedes roadster pulled into the parking garage eight hours later. Chase yawned and stepped from the vehicle. She wasn't in the mood to get into a fight. She'd listened to the ass chewing message that was left for her on her cell phone. She took a deep breath, walked inside the ten-story building and over to the elevator where pressed the button for the penthouse.

"Hey, I'm home." Chase kicked her flip flops off at the door. Yelena came around the corner to greet her. She stood about two inches taller than Chase.

"It's about fucking time. I haven't seen you in two weeks and then you decide to work instead of picking me up. Thanks a lot, Chase. I love you too." Yelena stomped into the kitchen.

"Damn it, Yelena. You know I'm always on call. Give me a break; I'm already working a hundred fucking hours a week. Forgive me if I decided to go save someone's life instead of carrying your goddamn suitcase!" Chase slung the refrigerator door open.

"I was going to wait for you, but I had no fucking idea when you'd be home, so I ordered my own dinner."

"Gee thanks. I figured you'd think only about yourself." She slammed the door shut, not feeling like cooking for herself. She grabbed her car keys and headed towards the front door.

"Where the hell are you going?"

"To get something to eat." Chase shook her head.

"Where?"

"Does it fucking matter? Rainer's probably, why?" Chase was trying not to raise her voice, but Yelena knew how to push her buttons.

"That's great! Go play with your goddamn friends. Your girlfriend's been gone for two weeks, and you go hang out with them. That's just like you, Chase!"

Chase yawned for the third time since she'd been home. "I'm not in the mood to argue with you. Fine you want to be mad at me go ahead. What's new?" She stormed out of the condo and headed towards the parking garage. She opened her cell phone and dialed a number as she got into her car.

"Hey."

"Are you busy?"

"No. Just watching TV and putting slides together for the show next week. What's up?" Frankie asked.

"I'm starving and I need to vent. I was headed to Rainer's, but if you want some company I'll stop by."

"Sure, I'll order a pizza."

***

Chase was sitting on the floor across from Frankie with an empty pizza box on the table between them, along with a pair of empty beer bottles.

"I can't believe she said that. She's such an asshole," Frankie said as she continued to examine the art slides that she had spread out all over the floor.

"Tell me about it. Sometimes I don't know why I'm still with her."

"It's called sex, honey."

Chase gasped. "That's even gone downhill. I remember when we first got together two years ago. We had more sex than I could keep up with, now I'd rather work than have sex with her."

"Why?"

"She used to be wild and willing you know. It didn't matter when or where, we just did it when we wanted to. Now, it's all about her. She wants to go to the clubs and bars so she can be everyone's eye candy. I swear she gets off on watching me fighting with people over her. I'm sick of it, Frankie."

"I'm sorry, that sucks. Have you tried to talk to her?"

"She only thinks about herself. When I try to talk to

her, she turns everything around on me. She just wants to be on the arm of a rich doctor, I don't even think it matters if I'm a man or a woman."

"When's the last time you made love, not had sex?"

Chase stared at the floor. "I... I don't think I've ever made love to her. It's always been hot and heavy, straight to the point sex."

"Hmm..."

"I bet she'd be nicer to me if I cut her ass off."

"Hell yeah, you give her a thousand dollar a week allowance, Chase. What did you expect? Of course, she's going to spend your money and treat you like shit." Chase knew Frankie was right.

"It's not quite that much."

"Well, it's definitely enough. Make her pay some bills or spend her *own* money for a change. Or better yet, kick her to the curb. Chase, you can do so much better than her."

"I've thought about it, I don't want to just put her out on the street though."

"I'm talking to you as your best friend, let her go."

"Whose work is that?" Chase asked as she started scanning the slides on the floor. Some of the artwork was beautiful abstract style sunsets and water scenes that she wouldn't mind taking a closer look at. Yelena had insisted on purchasing two very expensive Monet copies instead of the artwork that Chase actually liked.

"It's Remy Sheridan's. I'm featuring her in the show next week."

"Wow, some of these are gorgeous. She's very talented."

"Yeah. She'll be a major contender for one of my regular spots."

"What kind of prices are these going for?" Not that money was actually a problem. She just wanted to continue discussing the shy brunette.

"Probably three."

"Hmm…"

"What?"

"I was just thinking that's a hell of a lot less than I paid for those ugly-assed Monet's hanging in my foyer." They both laughed. "Don't get me wrong, I like art, but I'd much rather see one of these everyday than 'The Floating Ice' and 'Wheat Stacks.'" She laughed.

"Yeah," Frankie laughed again. "But, Chase, you do have two very valuable pieces of nice artwork."

"I love Monet's work, but Yelena has seriously bad taste. She chose them because of the price tag, I'm sure."

"Your right, she wouldn't know art if it slapped her across the face." They both laughed hysterically.

Frankie cleaned up the mess she had all over the living room floor as Chase cleaned up the pizza box and beer bottles.

"You look like a walking zombie. When's the last time you slept?"

"Last night."

"How long?"

"Uh…" She had to think about it. "Two hours."

"CHASE! You're going to kill yourself working like this."

The blond yawned and sat on the couch.

"Go get in the spare bed. She can wonder where you are all night, it's not like she's bothered to call you anyway. I'll wake you up in the morning." Chase didn't argue. She walked down the hallway and practically passed out as soon as she hit the bed.

***

Frankie walked into her spare room at six thirty a.m., Chase was already gone. She'd left a note saying she'd call her later since she was scheduled for surgery at seven a.m. By the time Frankie saw the note, Chase was already in surgery prep. She went straight to the hospital from Frankie's, neglecting her own house once again. She knew the inevitable was going to happen, she just wasn't prepared. Instead, she focused her mind on the operation she was about to perform, a quadruple bypass.

Six hours later she was finished and sitting at her desk listening to the multiple voicemails left by Yelena cussing her out.

"Wonderful, I love you too, bitch!" She decided to delete the rest of them after she heard the first three. *Pack your shit, 'French Bitch'.* She laughed.

***

Chase wasted no time when she walked in the door. Yelena was sitting on the couch watching TV. As soon as she began yelling, Chase cut her off.

"It's over, Yelena. It's been over for a while now. I want you out of here tomorrow."

"What! Excuse me, you stay gone all night then come home and tell me it's over and get out! Who were you out fucking all night, you piece of shit?"

"Yelena, first, you know better than that, I was at Frankie's. And second, we both know it's over. I'm sick of fighting with you, I'm sick of walking on eggshells in my own house, I'm sick of you, and I'm sick of us. I just want it to end. Please understand. I care about you, but I'm not in love with you."

"Fuck you!" Yelena went to slap her, but Chase caught her hand.

"Don't try me," she said between clenched teeth. "We can handle this like adults."

"Fine, you want me out, so be it. I've met someone anyway."

"Okay. At this point, Yelena, I don't really care." Chase went out to the hallway and brought in the empty boxes that she'd picked up on her way home. "Here." She tossed them on the floor. Yelena rolled her eyes and began packing up her belongings. Most of it consisted of clothing and shoes. Chase had basically given her twenty-four hours, but Yelena was packed and gone within four. She left with a loud slam of the door and the tires squealing on her BMW that Chase bought for her. Luckily it was paid off. She'd consider that a going away present.

Chapter 3

"I can't believe she threw her out like that," Gayle said as she took a glass of champagne from the waitress. They were standing in the middle of the Deluca Art Gallery for the show titled 'Past, Present, Future'. It was various artists that she had worked with for years, mixed in with some newer artists, and the feature of the night was her newest addition, Remy Sheridan.

"I'm sure she doesn't want to talk about it. She seems fine with everything though. Frankie said she's cutting her hours back at the hospital."

"That's good."

Chase walked behind them. "Gayle, Ping Pong, it's good to see you both." She hugged them. "Before you ask, it feels great to be single. It's over and the past is the past. According to Frankie, here's to the future." She held her champagne glass up.

"Well, you seem to be in a good mood." Ping smiled.

"I feel free, Ping. I haven't felt that in a long time." She grinned. "I'm going to walk around, come find me when you two are done gossiping about the crowd."

Secluded Heart

Chase walked towards the future section that featured the new artist. All of Remy's paintings were abstract, although most of them had a theme such as a sunset, the ocean, trees in a meadow, all with beautiful colors. Some of them were just a mixture of colors. Chase fell in love with the sunset over the ocean. She'd already purchased it from Frankie as soon as she saw it. Remy was told that painting was the first piece to sell, but she had no idea who'd purchased it. Frankie said the buyer wanted to remain anonymous. Chase continued to stare at the picture, wondering how it would look in her living room. She sensed someone nearby; her heart did a flip when she heard the familiar voice.

"Do you like it?" Remy asked. She was standing very close to Chase, behind her and a little to the side.

"It's amazing. I love what you did with the colors here and here." Chase pointed out, then turned to face the taller woman. She was eye level with Remy's nose. She didn't have to look into the brown eyes staring down at her; she could feel them on her.

"I'm glad you like it Doctor... uh... Chase." She smiled shyly; her eyes never faltered from Chase's. They were interrupted when a sandy-haired man appeared at Remy's side. He was a little taller than her. Chase backed up a little, putting some space between them. That's when she took a second to glance at Remy's outfit. She was wearing black slacks and a white sleeveless blouse. Her brown hair was messy like Chase's and too short to run a brush through.

"Sorry I'm late. I had a meeting than ran over." He kissed Remy's cheek. She flinched slightly from the contact. Chase only caught it because they were once again staring into each other's eyes.

"Chase, this is my boyfriend, Brian Martin. Brian, this is Dr. Chase Leery. She knows the owner and director of the gallery."

He stuck his hand out. She shook it respectfully and squeezed out a smile. "It's nice to meet you," he said.

"Likewise,"

"What kind of doctor are you?"

"I'm a cardiac surgeon." She glanced at Remy. Her brown eyes were glued to Chase's green ones. Chase could feel the heat from the stare penetrating her body. Her own heart fluttered nervously.

"Oh, here you are, Chase. I want you to meet Veronica Petrovski, she's another one of my artists." Frankie was standing there with a very pretty woman that was a bit taller than Chase, with long curly black hair and tan skin. *If this is a fix up, Frankie, I'm going to kick your ass, but she's definitely good looking.*

"Ronnie, this is Dr. Chase Leery."

"Hi, I've heard a lot about you." The woman smiled and offered her hand. Frankie continued to introduce Ronnie to Remy and Brian. Chase glanced up at Remy who was still staring down at her.

"If you'll excuse me, I need a refill." Chase backed out of the circle.

"Uh... I do too. I'll be right back." Remy turned to Brian then stepped away. Chase led them down the hall to Frankie's office.

As soon as she shut the door behind them, Remy pushed her up against the door and pressed herself against her. The anticipation was enough to drive them over the edge just before their lips met with a fiery passion. They wasted no time entering each other's mouth, letting their tongues taste one another. Remy's soft lips fit perfectly against Chase's. They could feel the heat burning where every inch of their bodies were fused together against the door. Chase threaded her arms around Remy's neck and into the back of her hair. Remy's hands were under the back of Chase's shirt against her skin, kneading the muscles in her lower back as they continued passionately kissing. Chase pulled away slightly and playfully bit Remy's lower lip, a soft moan escaped her as she slid her tongue past Chase's lips.

Out of nowhere, Remy peeled herself away from Chase, who was flat against the door. "I… we…" She stared into Chase's eyes one last time and flew out of the room like she was on fire. Chase took a second to catch her breath and proceeded down the hall. She caught up with one of the waitresses and grabbed two champagne glasses. She downed the first and put it back on the tray. She walked across the gallery with the other glass in her hand.

"Where have you been, young lady?" Ping grabbed her arm.

"Uh… I was looking at the paintings. Why?"

"Frankie's looking for you."

Oh." Chase saw the auburn-haired woman across the room talking to a couple of potential buyers. "I think she's trying to set me up with someone."

"I saw the woman you're talking about, she's hot."

"Who's hot?" Gayle walked up on the conversation.

"No one."

"The woman Frankie's trying to set Chase up with."

"I don't need to be set up with anyone. I just ended a two-year relationship a week ago. I'm not ready to heat up the sheets again."

"Uh huh, I think you have your eye on the straight new artist."

"What? Who are you talking about?"

"The one who is staring a hole through you."

Chase didn't have to turn around; she knew who Gayle was talking about.

"She's straight."

"So?"

"You know me better than that. Besides, I've talked to her a few times, she's really nice. I bought one of her paintings."

"You did?" Ping looked surprised. "Will it go with the others?"

"No, I'm thinking of selling them, I didn't want them in the first place."

"Didn't you pay a lot for them?"

"It's only money, Ping Pong," Chase laughed. "I'm sure I'll break-even; I would rather have her work hanging in my house anyway."

"I think you have a crush on her," Gayle snickered.

"Suit yourself." Chase rolled her eyes. Her lips still tingled from the make out session or whatever the hell it was they had in the office. She told herself if it wasn't for them being around all these people and in Frankie's office at the time, they more than likely would have gone a hell of a lot farther.

Chase saw Remy standing with Brian on the other side of the room talking to various people. The brunette continued to gaze at her with lustful eyes. *She's so damn adorable, ugh! Why does she have to be straight? That's my luck. And what the hell was that office episode about? I was really going to get another glass.* Frankie tapped her shoulder, bringing her out of the daze she was in.

"Huh?"

"Where did you go? You disappeared on me."

"Sorry, I was uncomfortable."
"What did you think of Ronnie?"
"Who? Oh yeah, she's pretty."
"She wants to get to know you better."
"That's nice."
"What's up? You're acting funny."
"Nothing's wrong." Chase shrugged her shoulders. "I'm fine. I don't think I'm ready to be set up with anyone though."
"That's fine. I just wanted to introduce you two. I think you'd be good together."

Chase took a deep breath. She couldn't get the earlier events off her mind. Every time she licked her lips, she felt Remy's mouth on hers. It wasn't helping when she'd look in the direction of Remy's paintings, the taller woman was looking back at her.

"Hey, Frankie, I think I'm going to head home."
"Are you okay?"
"Yeah, my head's hurting. I've had a long week."
"Hmm... I still think something's up with you. Go home and get some sleep. I'm sure it's quiet around there now."

"Yes, it is." Chase smiled and hugged her friend. She started towards Gayle and Ping who were standing close to Remy and Brian.

"I'm heading home, I've got a headache and I'm tired. I'll see you guys tomorrow for brunch at Rainer's."

Ping wrinkled her nose. "I'm sorry you're not feeling good, honey."

"Yeah, me too." She hugged them bye and turned towards the door. Remy was with Brian talking to a woman about one of the paintings displayed near the doorway. She'd have to walk past them to leave. *Damn it, so much for a clean getaway.*

Chase stopped next to them. "It was good to see you again, Remy. I'm looking forward to seeing more of your work." Chase stuck her hand out. She felt a burst of electricity when their hands touched. They held each other's hand a second too long, but no one noticed. "It was nice meeting you, Brian." Chase shook his hand briefly and put her best *eat shit* smile.

Chapter 4

Chase parked her roadster in the parking garage on the third floor and took the elevator down to the first-floor entrance of the hospital. She waved at various physicians that she passed on the way up to the cardiology floor where her office was located.

"Good morning, Dr. Leery."

"Hi, Jimmy. How are you?" She spoke to the male nurse who worked cardiology. He seemed to always be in the lounge when she went in for coffee. She wondered if he ever worked. Chase was still dressed in her business suit due to the regularly scheduled Monday staff meeting. Her cell phone began ringing on her belt before Jimmy could engage her in conversation. "Excuse me." She stepped into her office and answered the phone.

"Frankie? I didn't know you could get up this early," she laughed.

"I can be at work before seven a.m. if I want to."

"I see, so what do I owe the pleasure?"

"I need to talk to you. Can you come by the gallery at lunch time?"

"I have a staff meeting this morning, they usually

last about four or five hours. Is it urgent?"

"Yeah, I need to talk to you as soon as possible."

"Are you okay?" Frankie heard the concern in Chase's voice.

"Yeah, I'm fine. I just need to talk to you about something."

"Wanna meet at Rainer's?"

"No, I'd rather meet at the gallery. I have a lot of work to do today."

Chase was sitting behind her small wooden desk. She turned on the computer to check her notes for the meeting since she was supposed to speak on one of the topics. "Okay, I'll see you when I finish here." She hung up the phone wondering what was going on with Frankie. Maybe she met someone. She only acted funny when something was on her mind. *Hmm... oh well. I guess I'll find out later.*

***

"Okay, Frankie. What's up? You have me on pins and needles," Chase said as she walked into the office area of the gallery.

"Step into my office." Frankie turned towards her secretary. "Hold my calls, I'm in a meeting." She shut the door and walked towards her desk. Chase was already sitting in one of the leather chairs. Frankie walked in front of her and leaned back against the desk.

"I know what's going on with you."

"Huh?" Chase was confused. Frankie turned her computer screen around and pressed a button the mouse; suddenly, a small video of her and Remy against the door appeared from start to finish. The coloring quickly drained from Chase's face. She stared blankly at the screen. *Oh my god.*

"Care to explain?" Frankie said with a touch of sarcasm.

"I... I'm sorry Frankie, I had no idea."

"Well, neither did I until I checked my security cameras on my computer this morning, like I always do. How do you think I felt when I saw this? She's straight, Chase. You met Brian."

"I know." She wanted to crawl into a hole and hide. "Did you watch it? She's the one who shoved me against the door."

"Yeah, I saw it. A few more times that I would have liked to, and you didn't exactly push her off of you, as I do seem to recall."

"What do you want me to say?"

"I knew you were attracted to her, but this... what if he finds out, Chase? What if she drops you like a bad habit?" Frankie threw her hands into the air out of frustration.

"Nothing else happened."

"This is why you weren't feeling good wasn't it?"

"Yeah, I'm sorry I didn't just tell you."

"Have you talked to her since then?" Frankie moved around to her desk chair and sat down. She closed the camera window on the computer screen.

"No. We didn't exactly exchange numbers." She said with a grin. "You didn't show her this did you?"

"No. I wanted to call you both in here, but you're my best friend and I can talk some sense into you, so I don't plan on showing this to her."

"Good, can you delete it?"

"I just did." She smashed a few keys on the

keyboard. "Seriously, Chase. What are you going to do about this?"

Well, I'd like you to give me her number so I can call her. Then, I'd like to take her to dinner, but most of all, I want to lie on my balcony making love to her under the stars and listening to the waves crash until the sun comes up. "Nothing."

"You practically got it on with this woman against my office door and you don't care?"

"We didn't get it on, and what am I supposed to do, Frankie, she's straight!" She was back to wanting to crawl into a hole and hide.

"The worst part is I don't even know what to say about it. Just be careful, okay."

"I will. I doubt I'll even see her again, at least until she's in another show. Did you tell her I bought a painting?"

"No. Did you want me to?"

"No." Chase sat back in the chair. "Am I free to go warden?" she laughed.

"Ha." Frankie shook her head and laughed. "I still can't believe you two didn't get caught." Chase grinned and raised an eyebrow, as if to say she was too good to get caught.

"I have another meeting to get to at the Heart Institute." Chase stood up.

"You know, I haven't noticed you yawning as much. You must be sleeping."

"Yeah, I'm not being yelled at constantly." She shrugged.

"That's good. Has she tried to contact you?"

"Nope,"

"Have fun at your meeting, hot shot." Frankie rolled

her eyes and chuckled. Chase smiled. Frankie hadn't seen her best friend do anything of this nature since long before she met Yelena.

***

Sunday arrived before they knew it. Frankie, Gayle, Ping, and Chase sat at their usual corner table at Rainer's for brunch. Chase was wearing khaki shorts, a white tank top and flip flops. Her sunglasses were up on her head. The Miami heat was beating down close to a hundred degrees outside.

"So, where'd you put that painting you bought?" Ping asked.

"It's in the living room. Why?"

"Speaking of paintings, here comes your artist." Gayle saw Remy walk in. Chase turned her head and they immediately made eye contact. The gaze didn't break until Remy stopped at the counter to order her coffee.

"Go talk to her, Chase." Ping smacked her leg under the table.

"She's *your* artist, Frankie. You call her over," Gayle said.

"Leave her alone, girls," Frankie laughed and shook her head.

As soon as Remy was handed her coffee, she turned around to face their table. She and Chase made eye contact for a long moment before Remy left the restaurant.

"I'll be right back." Chase jumped up from the table and hurried towards the door. Frankie shook her head and frowned. She was worried for her friend. Straight girls were always trouble.

Chase looked both ways when she stepped out onto

the sidewalk. Remy was nowhere to be found. Then, she noticed a door closing on a white BMW 300 series. She ran towards the car and saw Remy sitting behind the wheel in the driver's seat. Remy started the car and rolled the window down halfway.

"Hi." Chase spoke first.

"Hey." Remy's chocolate brown eyes were sparkling in the sunlight. She was holding her sunglasses. Chase figured she caught her as she was about to put them on.

"Can we talk?" Chase put her hand on top of the car.

"I... I'm running late." She broke eye contact. "I'm supposed to meet Brian."

"Okay."

"I can't do this... I'm straight... I'm sorry." She rolled the window up and backed out of the parking spot.

Chase stood on the sidewalk cursing up and down. "Goddamn it!" *You got yourself into this, Leery!* She walked back into the restaurant trying to hide the frustration on her face.

"Did you catch her?" Gayle asked.

"No. She was already gone."

"She's so shy."

"You were shy when I first met *you*, Ping Pong," Frankie laughed.

"Yeah, but look at her now!" Gayle added and Ping smacked her arm.

Chase was glad the conversation wasn't about her anymore. "Let's go out Friday night."

"Where?"

"I don't know. I'm sure after this week I'll be in the mood to get drunk and dance until my old ass can't walk the next day." *I will do anything to get that woman out of my head.*

***

Friday arrived as slowly as possible. Chase was in surgery just about every day, but she had cut her hours back to eighty, which was a big change from one hundred the month before. All the girls met at Lucy's, a gay/lesbian night club in South Beach. *Wild Thing* was playing on the speakers when they walked in. Chase was in a black halter top and jeans; Ping was in a white halter top and jeans. Frankie was in a sleeveless blouse and khakis and Gayle was in jeans and a spaghetti strap top. They strutted together through the large crowd towards the bar.

"I'll have a dirty martini." Frankie ordered first.

Ping followed her. "I'll have a margarita, no salt."

Gayle ordered a beer. Chase stepped up behind her. "I'll have a double Jack on the rocks."

"Damn, Chase, anything we need to know about?" Gayle wiggled her eyebrows. "You're serious tonight."

"I just ordered a stiff drink. I didn't light up a joint, gees." They all laughed.

As soon as Chase grabbed her drink from the bar she felt a presence behind her, she turned almost into the arms of a very tall, broad woman wearing a wife beater and jeans. Chase wanted to run like hell.

"She's with me." Gayle put her arm around Chase and pulled her onto the dance floor. They began dancing to the *Wild Thing* song that was still playing. Chase mouthed 'thank you' to Gayle. Gayle smiled and continued to dance with her. If you didn't know any better, you'd think they actually were together by the way they danced with each other. One night a few years ago they did get a little drunk and sleep together. They had a brief relationship afterwards, but realized they were better off friends. They were far from being each other's type.

"You know, if these girls knew you were a doctor, you'd have to beat them off of you with a stick," Gayle whispered to her during a slow song.

"I know, thank god I've never run into any of them at the hospital."

"What would you do if your artist chic walked in the door?" Chase broke away and turned towards the door. "I knew it! You're serious on her, aren't you?"

"Damn it, Gayle. I don't want to talk about it okay. She's straight and nothing is going on with us. Besides, she won't even let me get close enough to say hi to her, much less anything else."

Two hours later, the ladies were starting to sober up after their drunken dancing fit. Ping rode with Gayle, so they left together. Frankie walked out with Chase since their cars were parked down the street.

Chapter 5

The following week Chase was on her way back to her office after completing an eight-hour triple bypass and mitral valve repair. She'd come to work in dark blue scrubs that morning because she was in surgery all day with no consults. She was happy to be in comfortable clothing and more than glad to see her day coming to an end when she sat in the chair behind her desk. Chase ran a hand throw her messy short hair and opened the charts that she needed to go over for her surgery appointments the next day. As soon as she turned off her computer there was a faint knock on her door. She looked down at her watch wondering who that would be.

"Come in," she said loudly. When the door opened her heart jumped into her throat and her palms filled with sweat. She blinked two or three times to make sure she wasn't hallucinating. "Hi."

Remy was standing in the doorway in a pair of faded jeans and a thin white oxford shirt, with the buttons all open except for the ones covering her chest. Her short brown hair was worn messy like Chase's, and she looked sexy as hell. Chase could barely swallow. She stared into the big brown eyes gazing back at her as she stood and walked across the room towards Remy. The taller woman stepped inside and shut the door without taking her eyes away from Chase.

"I..." Remy tried to speak but the words wouldn't come out. Chase put her finger up to Remy's soft lips.

"Sshh." She removed her finger and pressed her lips to the very same spot. The kiss started slowly as their lips parted, allowing for their tongues to explore each other. Chase ran her hands up Remy's chest and around the back of her neck into her hairline. Remy wrapped her arms around Chase, running her hands under the thin scrub shirt against Chase's warm skin. They rocked into each other as the kiss went deeper. Chase felt her heart beating wildly as the moisture built between her legs. Remy broke the kiss and bent her head towards Chase's ear. She outlined it with the tip of her tongue and then blew on it lightly. A faint moan escaped Chase's lips.

Remy whispered. "Take me home with you." Chase looked up into her eyes.

"Where's..."

"Out of town," Remy spoke softly. Chase broke away and grabbed her keys from her desk.

They couldn't get to the parking garage fast enough. Remy was out first since she wasn't in physician parking which was up higher. She pulled out onto the main road behind the convertible Mercedes when she saw Chase wave. Chase had the top down since it was almost dark, and the sun wouldn't kill her. She drove along the busy streets until she reached the beachfront scene. Her large condo building came into view, and she pulled into the parking garage. Remy parked in the visitor's section and met up with Chase at the elevator in the corner.

They reached the top floor and Chase unlocked the door to her two-story condo. The foyer was Italian marble tile with Monet paintings on each side. She tossed her keys on the small table. Remy mimicked her and kicked off her shoes. Chase gave her a quick tour downstairs, consisting of her office, the kitchen and living room, a spare room, and a full bathroom. Remy stopped dead in her tracks in the living room when she saw her own painting on the wall.

"I bought it at your show."

"I…" Remy's breath caught in her throat.

"I asked Frankie not to say anything. I actually bought it before the show. I was at her house the night she put the slides together. I saw it and told her I had to have it. I had no idea who the artist was or the price. I found out it was yours at the show." Chase grabbed her hand. "Come on there's more." She took her upstairs where there was another spare room and the master bedroom. A king-sized bed sat in the middle of the room, surrounded by a matching modern looking black and gray bedroom set. Chase kicked off her sneakers next to the closet door. She turned back towards the woman that was gazing into her eyes from across the room.

"I've… never done this," Remy whispered.

"We don't ha—"

Remy closed the distance between them and pressed her lips against Chase's. Once again, their tongues were tangled together as they kissed passionately. Chase reached between them, unbuttoned the rest of Remy's shirt, and let it fall to the floor. Remy pulled Chase's scrub top over her head and dropped it behind her. They removed each other's bra at the same time. Chase ran her hands tenderly over Remy's chest. Remy threw her head back when Chase put her mouth on one of her small breasts. She teased the dark nipple until it was hard in her mouth, then she blew on it, causing Remy to moan softly. Chase pushed Remy back towards the bed and removed her jeans and panties when she sat back, then she pulled her own scrubs and panties down and kicked them behind her. The blinds were slanted open allowing the moonlight to fill the room, casting a white glow over them. As Chase crawled on top of Remy, she slid her wet center along Remy's thigh.

"You do that to me," she whispered seductively as she bit Remy's lower lip. Remy pulled Chase against her tightly and traced her tongue around Chase's lips. Chase broke the kiss and moved down very slowly placing light kisses on Remy's tan skin from her breasts to her flat stomach. Tiny goose bumps rose on Remy's delicate skin.

Chase rubbed her cheek against the soft skin of Remy's inner thigh and continued to place tiny kisses as she worked her way towards the glistening patch of thin hair. Chase spread the folds with her mouth so slowly Remy thought she'd explode before she was actually touched. Her entire body quivered with anticipation. As Chase ran her tongue around the edge of the throbbing clit, Remy grabbed a hand full of her short hair and arched her back. Chase buried her tongue deep inside of her, then ran it over the bundle of nerves as she slid two fingers easily inside Remy. She felt the muscles tighten around her as Remy moaned softly. Chase sucked, licked, and stroked fast, then slow, hard then soft, until Remy could no longer hold back the orgasm that exploded deep within her. She held onto Chase's hair with one hand and grasped the bed sheets with the other. Chase wasted no time kissing her way back up to meet Remy's sweet mouth. Remy tasted herself on Chase's tongue as they kissed each other with profound emotion. Their shadows merged as one in the moonlight against the wall.

    No words were spoken as Remy placed sensual kisses on Chase's ear and down her neck. She sat up and straddled Chase as her hands began caressing both of her breasts. She bent to kiss them both and ran her tongue over the hard pink nipples. Chase gasped and held her breath as Remy moved further down her body. Remy held nothing back as she used her mouth to spread the folds and run her tongue through the wetness. She looked up at the sparkling green eyes gazing at her. Chase wanted nothing more than to feel this woman inside of her. As if she heard the words in Chase's heart, Remy slid her fingers inside of Chase as she continued to tease the swollen clit with her tongue. Chase arched her back and reached her arms out to the side tugging on the sheet as she lost herself in the waves of orgasm. Her heart pounded fiercely as she tried to swallow past the knot in her throat. Remy moved back towards her, and Chase took her chin in both hands. Their lips met tenderly once again. Chase wrapped her arms around Remy and held her tightly as they fell asleep tangled together.

***

    Chase woke up around midnight when she realized something warm was wrapped around her. She opened one eye to peak at the body beside her. Remy's head was just below her shoulder. Chase smiled and lightly kissed her forehead. Part of her wanted to thank god for bringing this beautiful woman into her life, and the other part of her was scared to death. She closed her eyes and breathed in the mixture of Remy's scent mixed with their lovemaking.

    Chase's alarm went off at four a.m. Remy sat up like someone had slapped her. Chase quickly turned off the annoying device. "I'm sorry."

"What time is it?" Remy stared around the room. It was pitch black outside.

"Four. I have a scheduled surgery at six." Chase looked into her eyes trying to read some kind of signal. "You don't have to get up, just lock the knob and pull the door shut on your way out."

Remy pulled the sheet up over her bare chest. Chase leaned towards her, their lips met in a passionate kiss, leaving both women breathless. Chase swore inside for having to go to work and leave this incredible woman in her bed. She got up and headed towards the shower while Remy lay back down and closed her eyes.

A half hour later, Chase was dressed in a fresh set of dark blue scrubs and black sneakers. She leaned over Remy and gently kissed her lips. Remy stirred but continued to sleep. Chase smiled as the image tugged at her heart.

Chapter 6

"Good morning, Dr. Leery," the nurse said as she helped Chase get prepared for the operation.

"That it is, Cathy. That it is." Chase smiled as the image of Remy in her bed came into view behind her eyelids. She opened her eyes to see her assistant for the surgery walk into the prep room. Every operation was different, she worked with a group of six surgical nurses and three cardiac surgeons of different levels, some were interns, and others were attendings. They only had two resident cardiac surgeons on staff since it was considered a teaching hospital.

"Good to see you again, Dr. Leery," the attending said as he stepped over to the sink.

"You too, Henry." Dr. Henry Grainger was a black man that was probably a few years older than her, and definitely a couple inches taller. Nothing intimidated her. She seemed to be the friendliest surgeon in the entire hospital, and everyone was pleased to work with her. She waited until he was all set, then she said her little prayer to herself and pushed the double doors open with her back. "Here we go."

The elderly white man was lying on the metal table covered with a heavy blanket from the waist down. A thin paper sheet covered his chest. Various wires and hoses stuck out from his face, chest, and right hand where he was attached to a ventilator, an IV line, and an EKG machine for monitoring his heart rate. Dr. Grainger inserted his endotracheal tube while Cathy, the red headed nurse, began opening the sterile packages of surgical instruments.

***

Three quarters of the way into the eight-hour valve replacement and bypass surgery, the patient's heart rate dropped suddenly, and then began beating rapidly. All three of them rushed around trying to control the erratic beating of the man's heart. His chest cavity was pried open, and his heart was in the middle of being repaired in various stages.

"Bag him!" Chase yelled to the other surgeon as the nurse brought the defibrillator paddles to her. Chase inserted the two thin metal spatula shaped paddles into the man's chest, one on either side of his heart.

"Charge!" she yelled. The nurse turned the machine up to two hundred. "Clear!" Chase yelled as she pushed the button to shock the heart. The varying rhythm continued, and then it stopped completely. Dr. Grainger continued to squeeze the bag, forcing oxygen into the patient's lungs.

"Three hundred!" Chase yelled and repositioned the paddles as the nurse turned the dial up. "Clear!" She shocked the heart again. The monitor was still showing a straight line and a loud steady tone continued form the speaker of the machine. "Goddamn it! Come on!" Chase removed the paddles and began massaging the man's heart with her gloved hands, trying everything she could to bring the organ back to life. Five minutes had passed on the wall clock. It was a hospital rule that after five minutes resuscitation stopped. "Go to four hundred, Cathy!" Chase yelled and stuck the paddles back into the man's chest. The nurse obeyed and turned the dial even higher. The machine made a loud buzzing noise, but the large muscle never moved.

Chase set the paddles down and backed away from the man. She looked up at the other surgeon. "Call it, Dr. Grainger." She pulled her gloves off and tossed them into the hazardous waste bin.

Henry looked at the clock. "Time of death is twelve thirty-two p.m." He pulled the spreader out of the chest cavity and closed the rib cage. Then he pulled the tube out of his chest and laid it on the instrument tray. Cathy pulled the sheet up, covering the man completely.

Chase took the rest of her covering off and left the room. As soon as she washed her hands and splashed water on her face, she took a deep breath to pull herself together. *Here comes the hard part.* She never understood why people died. No procedure was ever the same. Luckily for her, this was only the second patient she ever lost on her table. She'd grieve later. Right now, she needed to go tell the man's family.

***

Chase left the critical care waiting room. She proceeded down the hall and took the back stairwell to the rooftop of the hospital. The emergency helicopter was gone so she was all alone. The tears fell before she was able to move from the doorway. She didn't try to stop them, as this was only her body's natural way of handling the loss of a life in her hands. This was also only the second time that she'd cried in at least fifteen years. The only other time was the very first person she lost during another open-heart procedure in her attending year. This time, like the time before, it was an elderly man in very critical condition and his family wanted to do everything they could to get a few extra years out of his heart since he wasn't able to be put on the donor list.

The tears continued to fall as Chase sat with her legs crisscrossed on the concrete helicopter pad. She stared up towards the sky, the bright Florida sun was beating down on her, causing her to perspire. The pager clipped to her scrub pants buzzed. She checked to make sure it wasn't an emergency. It was the surgical Chief of Staff. *Great. Pull yourself together, Leery.* She sniffled one last time and wiped her face. She decided to stay out there a little longer before going to face her boss.

***

The large square office felt stuffy when she walked in and sat down. Dr. Paul Kellogg sat behind the desk. His grayish brown hair was shaved close to his balding head. He was wearing a lab coat over his dress pants and tailored shirt.

"How are you holding up, Dr. Leery?" He spoke with a deep voice.

"I'm fine, considering the circumstances." She did her best not to look grim.

"I need you to give me your statement. Cathy Pierce and Dr. Henry Grainger have already given me theirs." He handed her a packet of papers to fill out. "I want you to go fill these out in your office and bring them back to me.

After that..." He looked at her swollen eyes. "Go home and take a deep breath, Chase."

"I..." She took the packet off the desk and decided against finishing her shift. "Thank you." She was glad he suggested it, but more like ordered it.

***

It took over an hour for Chase to fill out the forms documenting the surgery and events leading to the patient's death. Afterwards, she returned it to Dr. Kellogg and left for the day. She decided to go ahead and clear her schedule and take the next day as a personal day.

As soon as she reached the garage, she remembered the beautiful way her morning had started out. "Talk about a one hundred and eighty degree turn around. I guess with pure heaven, you must encounter some kind of hell," she said as she got into her car. She dialed her home number, but the machine picked up. *Yeah, like she's still going to be there at three o'clock, you dumbass.*

Chase dialed another number on her cell phone and placed the speaker on as she backed the car out of the parking spot. On the third ring a high-pitched bubbly voice answered.

"Hello, Deluca Art Gallery. How many I help you?"

"Can I speak with Francis Deluca, please?"

"Yes, may I ask who is calling?"

"Chase Leery,"

"Oh, hello, Dr. Leery. I'll let her know it's you. Hold on for just a moment." Chase rolled her eyes and waited for Frankie to pick up.

"Dr. Leery, Ms. Deluca is on the other line. She said she'd call you back as soon as she can."

"Okay thanks." Chase hung up the phone and turned towards the beach. She was glad she only worked a few miles from home. That made the long hours somewhat bearable, knowing she could be home in fifteen minutes. Part of her hoped the beautiful brunette was still in her bed, at least, that thought counter acted the sadness she was still feeling.

When she walked in, she found a note lying on her dresser. She was glad she decided to go change clothes and not just crash on the couch, she wouldn't have seen the note for hours.

Chase,

I'm sorry. I don't know what else to say to you. This was a mistake. I can't see you again. Please don't try to contact me. I'm very sorry. I never wanted to hurt you. I made a stupid mistake and I'm sorry.

Remy

Chase saw a couple of tiny water marks on the paper, obviously from tears. She read over the short note at least ten times, before her cell phone rang.

"Hey," she said in monotone as she walked into the living room and plopped down on the couch.

"What's up?" Frankie asked.

"Where do I start?" Chase said sarcastically.

"Huh? What's wrong, Hun? Start from the beginning."

"Well, my morning began wonderfully, and then a patient died on my table…"

"Oh my god, Chase. I'm so sorry."

"Thanks. To make matters worse, I came home to a

note."

"A note from who?"

"The adorable woman I woke up with this morning. Apparently, it was a mistake on her part."

"Who? What woman? You're not back with Yelena, are you?"

"Hell no! I..." *Oh shit.* She realized she was about to let the cat out of the bag.

"Well?"

"What time are you leaving work?"

"Uh... I can leave now."

"Good, I don't feel like being alone right now."

"I'm on my way."

Chase closed her phone and tossed it on the table as she kicked her sneakers off and curled up on the sofa. She didn't have the courage to walk back into her bedroom and see the rustled sheets again.

A half hour later, Frankie was knocking on the door. Chase jumped up to let her in. "I'm so sorry, honey." Frankie threw her arms around her. She wasn't sure what else to say, they'd been friends for almost seven years. Frankie had never heard of Chase losing a patient. At least, she never talked about it before now.

They moved from the foyer into the living room. Chase sat on the couch and put her sock covered feet up on the table. Frankie sat next to her and put her feet up too.

"What happened, Frankie? I don't understand, one minute I was stitching a bypass and the next he crashed. I did everything." Her voice cracked. "I massaged his fucking heart with my hands trying to bring him back!" The sadness was turning to anger.

"How old was he?"

"Seventy-five," she sighed. "He was critical, and his

heart wasn't going to make it much longer. His family wanted to get a few more years out of him so they opted for a major operation, one that involves surgical procedures that I do every day."

"Well Chase, he was seventy-five and in bad shape. His chances probably weren't that great to begin with."

"I know, but he shouldn't be, Frankie!" Frankie grabbed her hand and squeezed it.

"It's not your fault."

"I know. I have to go in front of the medical board after they review the file."

"That sucks."

"Yep, but that's medicine for you. It's also the reason I carry a personal million-dollar malpractice insurance policy."

"I'm sure it won't come to that."

"I hope so," she said, knowing she did everything accurately.

"Hmm..." Frankie smacked her thigh. "So, who's the woman that broke your heart today?"

Chase wanted to crawl in a whole. "I ..." *Shit*.

"Spit it out, Chase. Who is she?"

I can't lie to her. If I did and she found out, she'd never forgive me. "Remy Sheridan."

"Oh my god, Chase." Frankie was hysterical. "You slept with her!? Oh my god!"

"Calm down." Chase stood up and walked over to the liquor cabinet by the wall. "I need a drink. Want something?"

"The stiffest thing you have in there, make it a double. Damn it, Chase. I thought there was nothing between you two."

Chase walked back over to the couch with two neat

glasses of whiskey. "So did I." It only took two sips to empty the glass. "I don't know. Everything happened so fast."

"How? How the hell did she end up in your bed?" She finished her own glass. "Where the hell was Baron or Brian or whatever the fuck his name is?"

"Out of town." Chase sat back on the soft leather sofa. "She's so damn shy. We haven't said more than three or four words at a time."

"Okay?"

"I don't know, Frankie!" Chase yelled. "She told me to stay away from her when we were at Rainer's, then she shows up at the hospital and is all over me again. She asked me to take her home."

"So, you do! What the fuck, Chase."

"I…" *Goddamn it.* "I don't know. I'm very attracted to her."

"That doesn't mean you bring her home and fuck her Chase!"

"It wasn't like that, Frankie! God, do you have to be so vulgar?"

"Well, how did it happen then?"

Chase closed her eyes and pictured the entire night and morning like it had just happened. She took a deep breath. "I brought her here and one thing led to another. It was so natural. I showed her around the house and the next thing I know we were in my bed." She stared at the painting hanging on the wall across from them. "Do you remember me telling you about Yelena?"

"What about her?"

"Sexually. Anyway, last night… Frankie, last night was the first time I've ever actually 'made love' to someone," Frankie saw the sadness in her best friend's eyes. "Probably the last time too."

"What happened with her?"

"I don't know. She left me a damn note saying she was sorry, but it was all a mistake."

"Man. When you step in shit, you really fucking step in it!"

"Gee thanks!"

They both laughed. "At least you're not in love with her." Chase turned away. "Oh no, Chase." Frankie shook her head.

"No. I'm not in love with her, but I could fall for her very easily."

"The best thing for you to do is stay away from her."

"I took tomorrow off. I need to clear my head before I go back to work." She took a deep breath and let it out slowly. "I really wasn't prepared for this when I got home. What a total cluster fuck."

"You can't fix everything, Chase. You're human, honey." Frankie put her arm around her. "Wanna get drunk and watch cartoons?"

"God, I haven't done that in years." They laughed. Chase refilled their whiskey glasses and turned the TV to the Family Guy.

***

Two hours later, they'd consumed at least four or five glasses of whiskey each.

Frankie was laughing hysterically. "I can't believe you found a marathon of this. I never watch it anymore."

"I know. Yelena hated it! I love Stewie, the baby. He's funny as hell."

"Brian, the dog, is a trip. I loved the episode where he dated Meg." Frankie was chuckling so hard she thought she'd pee her pants. Chase didn't forget about the events of her day, but she was doing a pretty good job of putting them in the back of her mind.

Chapter 7

A little over three months later, life was semi back to normal for Chase. Work was moving along as usual, and she finally let herself get over losing a patient on her table. She owed her group of friends for that. They seemed to be right there to cheer her up. She hadn't heard from or seen Remy. Chase seemed to be over it, but deep down she was hurting and was still furious with herself for getting involved with a straight woman to begin with.

"I can't believe it's already Thanksgiving. It's still a hundred goddamn degrees outside!" Gayle said as she ordered a chilled latte from the waitress. She was wearing a light green tank top and black shorts. The new girl she was dating sat next to her, but somehow, she didn't fit in with the group. Maybe it was because she was pasty white with freckles and orange red hair. The complete opposite of anyone Gayle had ever dated. She was usually with some of the hottest girls. Still, the group kept their mouths shut. Everyone seemed to learn from their mistakes with Chase after she told them about her heartbreaking episode with Remy. She threatened to tear their heads off anytime someone made a comment about it.

"I'll be glad when the holidays are over. I could care less about the weather; I'm used to sweating my ass off year-round. I'm from here, remember?" Chase laughed and took a sip of her coffee.

"What's the weather like in China, Ping?" the new girlfriend asked. Ping rolled her eyes. Chase spit a mouthful of coffee onto the table, nearly choking.

"I wouldn't know. I was raised in Florida, by white people." She raised an eyebrow, almost egging the girl to comment. But she didn't, instead she stroked Gayle's hand like she was some kind of animal with fur. Chase and Frankie both snickered.

"So…" Frankie sat back in her chair. "At Christmas I'll be having the Annual 'Best of the Year' show. The plan is for the week before Christmas, with that first Friday night being a large private showing and party."

"Cool." Ping smiled.

"I can't wait, I love mingling with the rich artsy people," Gayle said. "Have you ever been to an art gallery, Maureen?" she said to the girl sitting next to her.

"No. But, it sounds like a lot of fun!"

Great, Chase thought. *Not only will she be there.* Referring to the woman she was desperately trying to forget. *But Gayle's new flame will be tagging along. Absolutely wonderful. I can always fill my schedule to the gills, but I have to be there for Frankie. I guess I'm going.* She gave her best 'I can't wait' smile and raised her glass to toast the event.

***

Two weeks later, Chase was sitting in her office signing charts and setting her schedule. She had three more consultations to do before her day was over. She was glad to see Thanksgiving come and go. She'd spent the day with the girls at Frankie's house. Frankie made the turkey and everyone else brought some sort of side dish. Chase settled for squash casserole and was glad she still had her mother's old recipe. Gayle still had Maureen around. Everyone secretly wondered how long the little affair would last. Ping tried to coerce Chase and Frankie into putting money on it, but Chase refused. She'd already had her go 'round with Gayle, which actually happened by mistake. Therefore, she would feel bad about betting on how long Gayle would keep this girl around.

Of course, she still had the art show to consider. Chase wished for a way to get out of going. Seeing Remy was not something she was in the mood for. She'd almost rather fall into a rat-infested sewer drain naked. At least she'd have a reason to feel depressed. On the other hand, she couldn't really let her life come to an end over a one-night stand, so she decided to suck it up and go with a smile. It may be an 'eat shit' smile, but she'll still appear happy as if nothing ever happened between them. Surely, Brian or Barron or whatever the hell his name was, would be there on her side. One more reason for Chase to curse herself, not only was it a one-night stand where she practically fell head over hills like a lovesick teenager, but damn it, it had to be a straight woman with a boyfriend.

Chase continued to do her paperwork, at least work kept her head clear. She was back to working close to ninety hours a week when she volunteered at the Heart Institute. They always had some kind of seminar going on that they wanted her to speak at or be a part of in her spare time. *What spare time?* she thought.

Secluded Heart

***

"I can't believe they're still together," Ping said as she walked into the art gallery with Chase. "It's been what six, maybe eight weeks."

Who gives a shit, Ping?" Chase stated as she held the door open to the exhibit hall. "Gayle likes Maureen; maybe she found her soul mate."

"Ha. Leave it to you to get all sentimental and shit, Chase," Ping laughed.

"Are you jealous?"

"Hell no, have you seen her?"

Chase decided not to comment on Maureen's looks. "I'm only stating the obvious, Ping. Let it go. The next thing you know, Gayle will be single again and you'll be the one asking, 'where's Maureen?' I know how you work."

They walked towards the nearest waitress and grabbed a couple glasses of champagne. Frankie spotted them from across the room and immediately made a beeline in their direction.

"Hey guys." Frankie hugged them both. "I'm glad you're here."

"There you are. I lost you when we came in the door," Gayle said as she and Maureen met up with the group. Chase wasn't about to say, 'well we had to take a detour because Ping wouldn't keep her mouth shut'.

"Chase, Ronnie's here. She was asking about you."

"Ronnie?" Chase looked at her with a crooked stare.

"The girl she tried to set you up with last time," Ping announced. Chase was beginning to the think Ping needed to get laid. She was becoming a nuisance.

"Oh, I remember her. Where is she?"

"Come on, I'll take you to her." Chase followed Frankie into another section of the large, partitioned room.

Veronica Petrovski was as tall as Remy. Chase blamed it on the stilettos she was wearing. Otherwise, she figured she was only a little taller than Chase.

"Hi, it's nice to see you again," Ronnie said with a smile. Her curly, dark hair hung a little past her shoulders. She was wearing a crème-colored pantsuit with a salmon-colored blouse underneath. Her olive complexion contrasted perfectly. Chase had to admit the woman was beautiful.

"Likewise, Ms. Petrovski." Chase smiled back.

"Please, call me Ronnie." She winked.

Okay, this is off to a good start. Then Chase recognized the work on the wall next to Ronnie's. *Damn it.* Sure enough, Remy was standing in the middle of a small cluster of people who were admiring her art. When Chase saw the deep brown eyes gazing her way, she immediately turned back towards Ronnie. *You wanna play games, I can play your goddamn games, alright.* Chase offered to get Ronnie another glass of champagne. She quickly returned to find Remy watching her every move. She saw the tall sandy-haired man at Remy's side put his arm around her. She laughed at something he said, all the while staring in Chase's direction. *Jealousy is not the game you want to play with me 'Miss Thing'.* Chase smiled. *Game on.* She stepped closer to Ronnie and initiated conversation. Minutes later, they were walking around together. Ronnie had her arm in the small of Chase's back as she walked her around to each piece, explaining the lines and thought process behind each of her paintings that were on display. Remy saw the two of them finally leave the room together.

Ronnie took Chase to the back of the gallery into

another exhibit that was closed off because of the show that night. A few of her favorites were in this room. She showed Chase each one and continued to describe them to her.

"I'm very fond of you, Dr. Leery," she said with pride.

"Please, call me Chase." Ronnie reached out and stroked Chase's jaw with the back of her fingers. Chase flinched with the first touch of their skin. She felt terrible, here was this beautiful woman throwing herself at Chase and all she could think about was Remy. Using this woman to play Remy's twisted game of cat and mouse was not the smartest thing she'd ever done. Chase couldn't think fast enough as Ronnie leaned in and kissed her. Their lips met softly at first and then passionately parted to allow their tongues to taste one another. Neither of them noticed the woman in the doorway. She walked away before they parted.

"That was ... uh..." Chase fumbled for words.

Ronnie smiled. "It was nice. In fact, I'd like to do it again." She leaned in and kissed her once more. Chase didn't stop her. She seemed to welcome the contact and the embrace that followed. When Chase opened her eyes, she was in the woman's arms and inches from her face. She looked into the brown eyes staring at her. *The wrong brown eyes.* She thought to herself. *Damn it let it go.* Chase initiated the next kiss this time doing everything she could to push Remy from her mind.

When they parted again, Chase found her voice. "We should get back. I'm sure my friends are probably looking for me."

"Yes, you're probably right." Ronnie touched her cheek. "I'd like to see you again."

"I think I'd like that too." Chase spoke before she

thought about her words. *Hell, I wouldn't mind having meaningless sex with her. She's definitely better looking than Maureen.* Chase hid the snicker from her mind.

***

"Where the hell have you been?" Ping asked when she spotted Chase walking back into the open exhibit. Chase smiled. Frankie shook her head. At least she was off with Ronnie, another *lesbian* and a single one, for that matter.

"What did I miss?"

"Nothing, Houdini," Ping said with a sarcastic grin. Chase searched the room for Gayle and Maureen. She noticed them talking to a few people in the corner. Chase continued to scan the room. Remy was staring back at her and alone. *Now's your chance. Go in for the kill.* She thought to herself as she headed in Remy's direction, stopping to grab another champagne glass on her way through the crowd.

"Hey." Chase was lost in the chocolate brown eyes gazing at her. She'd never been able to feel so much of someone through their eyes. Her heart did a back flip and stuck in her throat.

"Hi." Remy's eyes never wavered.

"It's… uh… so… uh…" *Shit.*

"I… I didn't think you'd be here," Remy finally said as they continued to look into each other's eyes.

"Frankie's my best friend. I'm at all her shows."

"Yeah…" Remy tried to say something else, but Ronnie appeared at Chase's side.

"I lost you. Are you ready to get out of here?" Ronnie's voice was full of seduction as she placed her hand on Chase's back.

"I... uh..." *Checkmate!* Remy's eyes were questioning her. "Sure, let's go." She went to walk away with Ronnie, and then turned back towards Remy. "Good to see you again, Ms. Sheridan." She flashed her 'eat shit' smile and walked away. She closed her eyes as soon as she met the sweltering heat outside. One lone tear made its way down her cheek. She was thankful for the darkness. Ronnie didn't notice the brief show of emotion. Chase wiped her face and continued walking towards her car.

"Where are you parked?" Ronnie asked. Chase hit the keyless entry and the lights flashed on her Mercedes roadster sitting across the road. "Nice!"

"It gets me from Point A to Point B." Chase smiled ear to ear. That car, next to the oceanfront condo she lived in, was the only thing she ever splurged on for herself. The rest of her treasures were at the hands of Yelena. "Hey, I'm kind of hungry, would you mind if we just went to dinner? I don't think I'm going to be great company tonight." Honestly, Chase wanted to go back inside and smack Remy for making her fall for her. Although she was equally to blame, she let it happen.

"No, dinner's fine with me. I'll follow you."

Chapter 8

Chase was coming out of Rainer's after having her usual Sunday brunch with the group, when Remy was about to enter the restaurant at the same time. Their eyes locked. Chase's first instinct was to step aside and let her go by, but she decided against it.

"Can we talk?" She stepped onto the sidewalk outside of the entrance way to the door.

"Okay?" Remy was nervous, Chase could see it in her confused eyes.

"What's going on with you? I..."

"Did you sleep with her?" Remy blurted out.

"Huh? Who?" Chase furrowed her eyebrows, and then it clicked. Her little stunt must've worked. "No. But even if I had, what's it to you? You're the one with the *boyfriend*." Chase ran a hand through her own short hair. Neither woman broke eye contact. "Look I don't want to have an affair with a straight woman, much less one that's involved in a relationship."

"He's only my boyfriend, I'm not married."

"You're straight!" Chase raised her tone. "Or at least I thought you were."

"I *am* straight," Remy said.

"This is a losing situation for me." Chase shook her head.

Remy pushed her against the side of the building and kissed her. All rational thinking flew out of Chase's ears as she wrapped her arms around Remy and pulled the taller woman against her. The kiss took them both to new heights as their lips parted and tongues explored. A hot and heavy make out session wasn't what Chase pictured when she thought about confronting Remy on their situation, but she couldn't resist the pull this woman had with her or the way her entire body, mind, and soul opened to Remy just by looking into her eyes.

"I want you," Remy whispered in Chase's ear.

"God, I want you too!" Chase kissed her once again, leaving them both breathless. "I… Remy…"

"Take me home with you." Remy's brown eyes were glazed over with desire. Chase would be a fool not to go make love to this beautiful woman, but she'd be stupid to get deeper involved than she already was.

"We… what about…"

"Out of town," she said softly.

Chase forced herself to let go of the woman that fit perfectly against her. "Remy…" The taller woman tried to butt in. "Listen to me, please…" She pleaded with her as her own heart melted right there on that sidewalk. "I can't… I'm not going to do this, not unless I can have all of you. I'm not going to be another *mistake*."

"It's complicated," Remy said as a tear rolled down her face. Chase wiped the warm liquid from Remy's face and kissed her lips tenderly.

"Call me when it's not," Chase said flatly, and then she turned and walked away. She fought off the tears long enough to get into her car. They flowed like a waterfall as she drove away from the curb. *Goddamn it! Could my life possibly get any worse?*

Chase never saw the SUV run the red light to her left. The large red truck was headed straight for her, as she crossed the intersection it, t-boned the driver side of her Mercedes sending her little car careening into a parked car head on. The rollercoaster ride she was on came to a stop after the airbags deployed. What felt like minutes lasted only seconds. Chase hit the left side of her face on the door, causing a small cut and a huge bruise around her left eye. She was close to unconscious when a nearby witness raced over to check on her. Another passerby was already on the phone with nine-one-one.

"Are you okay ma'am?" the man asked. He couldn't reach her, but he smashed out the rest of the passenger window so he could at least see her. "Don't move. Help is on the way."

"I... m..." She tried to speak but couldn't form the words. Her head felt like someone put it in a vice. She closed her eyes.

***

As soon as the fire department finished cutting the tiny car like a tin can, they strapped Chase to a backboard and hauled her out of the twisted metal and into the back of the ambulance. The driver of the truck wasn't wearing his seatbelt, so he was thrown from the vehicle and died on the scene. He was drunk. You could smell the alcohol coming from the truck. He was speeding and never hit his brakes.

Before the ambulance left, Chase's cell phone started ringing and the policeman on the scene answered it.

"Excuse me?" Frankie said when she heard the deep male's voice on the other end. "I think I have the wrong number."

"Are you trying to reach... uh..." He looked at the name he scratched on his report. "Ms. Leery?"

"Yes, Dr. Chase Leery. Why do you have her phone?" She asked.

"She was involved in an auto accident."

"Oh my god! Is she okay? Where? What happened?"

"Calm down, ma'am. Are you family?"

"I'm..." Frankie thought quickly. "I'm her sister."

"She was just taken to Mount Sinai Hospital."

"How bad is it?" she questioned as she ran out the front door of her house. She'd left Rainer's before Chase, so she had time to make it home and never saw the accident. Ping and Gayle left right after Frankie. Chase stayed behind to answer a question Paul had about open-heart surgery. His mother lived in Connecticut and was told she needed to have a double bypass very soon. He was in the dark trying to understand the information the doctors gave his brother.

"I'm not sure, ma'am. She was alive when they pulled her from the car."

"Oh my god," Frankie choked back tears and hung up the phone. She dialed another number quickly as she drove on.

"Hey what's up?" Ping answered.

Frankie tried to talk between sobs.

"Huh? What's wrong, Frankie? I can't understand you, calm down."

"Chase!" She yelled.

"What about her?"

"She…" Frankie tried to pull it together. "She was in a car accident…"

"What?"

"I don't know Ping… the cop said… he said she was alive when they pulled her out of the car…"

"Oh my god! What! Oh my god! Where is she?" Ping was hysterical.

"Mount Sinai. I just pulled up. Call Gayle." She closed her phone and ran into the emergency room.

***

When the ambulance arrived, the paramedics wheeled the stretcher into the ER. The trauma resident didn't recognize her since she was covered in blood from the inch-long cut on her head and strapped to a backboard with a neck brace clamped to her head. The left side of her face was severely bruised, and her eye was swollen, almost shut.

"Her name's Chase…" The paramedic said to the doctor. "We pulled her out of a tiny convertible roadster. An SUV practically ran over her and squashed her into a parked car." They moved her onto a hospital gurney but left her strapped to the plastic board and in the neck brace. The doctor looked closely at her as he listened to her breathing and peeked behind the eyelid on the uninjured side of her face.

"Dr. Leery?" He turned towards the paramedics that were leaving the room. "What kind of car did you say that was?"

"Uh…" He looked at his notepad. "Some kind of silver sports car, I think maybe a Mercedes."

Suddenly, the doctor started yelling orders to the

nurses and the attending that was with him. "Call radiology and tell them we have a trauma code red NOW! She needs a CT scan, facial x-rays as well as head, neck, and chest x-rays!" Code red meant one of their own, sort of like top priority.

The paramedics noticed the immediate change of pace in the room. "Do you know her?"

"Yes, she's one of the best cardiac surgeons in Miami. She works here," he said as he helped wheel the gurney down to radiology. "How bad was it? Was she awake at all?"

"No, she was unconscious, but breathing on her own when we arrived. The witness said she was awake and tried to speak to him right after it happened. The car was unrecognizable. We had to practically cut around the driver compartment to get her out. It didn't cave in too badly on her legs though. The airbag probably hit her in the chest. We found her slumped against it and the door."

"My god." The trauma doctor shook his head and walked towards radiology.

***

"Excuse me, I'm looking for Dr. Chase Leery. She was brought here from a car accident." Frankie sounded winded; she'd run all the way from the parking garage.

"Um..." The nurse behind the desk checked the records. "I don't see her on here."

"Look, lady!" Frankie almost went over the counter. "She was brought here by ambulance, all..." The tears just wouldn't stop. "All I know is she was alive when they got her out of the car. She's a heart surgeon here, I'm sure you probably know her." The woman stood up.

"Wait just a minute." She walked away. Frankie paced the floor praying for Ping and Gayle to get there as quickly as possible. She wasn't sure she could handle seeing Chase alone.

"She's in radiology, that's all they can tell me. Are you family?"

"We all are," a sobbing voice answered from behind Frankie. Ping and Gayle were standing a few feet away crying their eyes out. The nurse looked at them quizzically. Here you have a woman with jet-black hair and semi-tanned skin, an auburn-haired woman with fair skin, and a short Asian woman. None of them looked related to each other and the only thing she could remember about Dr. Leery was she was tan and blond. Frankie caught on to the oddball stare. "We were all adopted," she said quickly.

The nurse shook her head. "Come with me, I'll take you to the family waiting room." She walked them down a ridiculously clean hallway with chalk white floors and baby blue walls. All three of Chase's best friends walked into the tiny room still crying.

"We saw the car," Gayle said as she sat on one of the hard gray chairs.

"What?" Frankie asked as she sat down next to her. Ping took the seat on the other side of Gayle.

"Ping picked me up on Seventh. I was at Cordova's looking for a birthday present for my Mom. Anyway, we rode past Rainer's on the way here. It must've happened right after she left. They were still cleaning everything up and the car was on a flatbed wrecker, along with a big red Expedition and a little black Acura." Gayle wiped the tears from her face.

"There was nothing left of her car, Frankie. It was a silver ball of metal with cloth mixed in from the convertible top and white airbags." Ping stared at the floor.

"Oh my god." Frankie closed her eyes and prayed silently for her best friend's life.

"I... uh... I took a couple pictures with my camera phone as we passed it," Gayle said half under her breath.

"That's fucked up, Gayle."

"What if... I don't know... I just took them, okay." Gayle felt bad enough as it was. She wasn't really thinking about Chase being hurt at the time. She was just amazed at the car.

"Well, at least let me see them," Frankie blurted with sarcasm. Gayle pushed a few buttons on her phone and handed it to Frankie.

"Holy shit! Oh my god, Chase." There were two pictures of the Mercedes and one of the truck and other car. Frankie's hands were shaking as she handed the phone back to Gayle. "She's..." Frankie closed her eyes. "She's lucky to be alive."

***

An hour later, the doors to the waiting room opened. "Hi, I'm Dr. Rosenthal. Are all of you with Dr. Leery?" The moderately short, brown-haired man stood in front of them in dark blue scrubs and a white lab coat.

"Yes. How is she? Can we see her?" Frankie stood up to speak to him. She was surprised to see that she was almost taller than he was.

"She's going to fully recover, but right now she has a concussion and a severe contusion to the left side of her face. She had a small cut above her left eye that took six stitches. Surprisingly, she didn't break any bones, but she'll be very sore for a while and have a hell of a black eye.

She's asleep at the moment, but it would be better for her to stay awake right now." He backed up a little bit. "If you come with me, I'll take you to her."

They walked down one hallway, and then turned down another. Gayle noticed the sign for Intensive Care and an arrow pointing in the direction they were heading.

"She's in here so she can be monitored frequently because of her concussion."

"How long will she be here?" Ping asked.

"At least 24 hours, but possibly 48, just to be on the safe side." He waved towards the open doorway. Frankie was the first one to walk in. Chase had IV lines coming from both hands and an oxygen tube stuck in her nose. Bright blue stitches stuck out from the dark bruising on the left side of her face. Her eye socket and cheek were severely swollen. Her blond hair had dried blood in it, but it looked like the nurses did their best to clean the blood from her face and neck. Frankie thought she looked peaceful laying there under the thick blanket sound asleep. She walked over and rubbed her fingers on her left hand. Chase never stirred.

"I'm so sorry, honey," Frankie whispered as the tears came back full force.

"At least she's okay. The Doctor said her eye will heal with no problem." Ping hugged Frankie.

"We're all here, Chase. We love you," Gayle said as she squeezed the fingers on Chase's right hand.

Chapter 9

Frankie brought Chase home from the hospital two days later. She stayed with her around the clock for the first couple of days since she was still in an extreme amount of pain and unable to do a lot for herself. Surprisingly, she didn't break any bones, but she felt as though she shattered her entire skeleton, she was hurting so badly. The pain pills knocked her out within minutes, so it was either stay awake in unbearable pain or take the pills and go to sleep.

"I need to go to the office and take care of some paperwork. I'll be back in a few hours. Take your pills and get some rest, honey."

"What day is it?" Chase asked groggily. She was unable to remember the accident. In fact, she couldn't remember much about Sunday at all, except for having a conversation with Remy and being sad.

"It's Friday. Why?"

"What's the date?"

"December twenty third." Frankie raised a questioning eyebrow. "Got a hot date for Christmas?"

Chase grinned. It hurt way too much to laugh. "Just a foursome with you, Ping, and Gayle." The girls had been together on the holidays for the past four years. Even if they were dating people they were always together. None of them were from Miami except Chase, and her family moved away to escape the heat, so the girls became each other's family. Demanding jobs and busy lives kept them from going to see their families in multiple states.

When Frankie was leaving there was a knock at the door. She opened it to a giant bouquet of various flowers in a crystal vase. Frankie figured the arrangement probably cost close to three hundred dollars. She took it inside and put it with the giant array of flowers that were sent to the hospital by co-workers and other friends. Chase's condo was starting to look like a flower shop with at least twenty arrangements scattered.

"That one's huge, who's it from?" Chase asked quizzically. She was lying on the couch watching reruns of CSI: Miami. For some reason she always got a kick out of watching it since she lived in Miami and there was no way in hell that show was taped there. To her it was like watching a mockery of her city. That and the fact that she slept halfway through every episode seemed to help. Plus, the women were usually good looking.

Frankie opened the card and walked over to the couch with it. Chase's face was still bruised badly. Her left eye was black and blue, and she still had stitches. She also had bruising on her chin and chest from the airbag. It literally looked like someone beat her up, but luckily for her, it was only bruising and a minor cut that would more than likely heal with no scar.

Chase took the card and flipped it open. Frankie stood in silence as Chase read the inscription.

Chase,

I'm glad you're okay. I went to the hospital to see you, but I didn't know what to say, so I never went inside. I've driven by your house a hundred times since I found out you came home, but I couldn't bring myself to stop. Anyway, I just wanted to say I'm sorry and I hope you get well soon.

Remy

Chase tossed the card onto the coffee table. "Did you tell her?"

"No." Frankie shook her head.

"Hmm…" Chase laid back down on the couch. As soon as Frankie was gone, she threw the TV remote across the room, it was the closest thing she could grab. The batteries flew out when it crashed against the wall.

"Goddamn you! What gives you the right to lead me around like your fucking puppet on a string?!" Chase still couldn't remember the accident, but she did finally start remembering the events of that day. In particular, the entire conversation she'd had with Remy, so lying helplessly on her couch staring at the enormous bundle of flowers on the table only pissed her off. Chase took a pain pill and went to sleep, at least this way she wouldn't sit around thinking about the woman who made her heart skip a beat and blood boil all at the same time. *Boy, what a cliché,* she thought.

***

Later that same night, Frankie, Ping, and Gayle all came over to Chase's. Frankie made homemade pizzas for dinner, and they sat around watching the movie version of

Rent on DVD. They seemed to do that anytime something was going on with one of them. Their 'Rent night' had become a karaoke singing fest. They each had a favorite character and could sing all the songs. Chase had to admit it cheered her up. She'd only thought about Remy once every half hour, instead of every ten minutes. Especially since the flower vase was nearby. Ping and Gayle went around and read all the cards. Remy's bouquet was the only one with no card and it was by far the most extravagant, so naturally they questioned her about that one.

"I thought she stayed with her boyfriend?" Gayle asked. Ping wanted to smack her in the back of the head for bringing it up.

"She's still with him. We uh... I... I ran into her when I left Rainer's..."

"When?"

"I guess right before the accident, I don't know. All I remember is basically telling her it was me or him."

"Wow and she sent you flowers? What did the card say?"

"It's none of your business, Gayle!" Frankie barked.

"No, it's okay. She just said get well soon. It was nothing special."

"The flowers she sent are gorgeous." Ping smiled.

"Yeah." Chase fought back a tear.

***

Two days after New Year's, Chase was back to work full time. Her black eye was gone, and she had a very thin little scar above her left eye from her stitches. Her bruised muscles were still sore and aching but all in all, she was back to normal. She'd already bought a new car.

Ironically, it was exactly like the one she'd totaled, the same slate gray exterior with a black convertible top and black leather interior. This one just happened to be two years newer than the other one and just as loaded.

Chase had just come out of a three-hour mitral valve replacement surgery when her pager went off. She decided to call the number back from her office phone since she was heading in that direction. She was a little tired from working just over eighty hours in the past week. When Chase put her mind to something, she did it. The entire cardiac staff, as well as the surgical staff tried to get her to come back slowly, that had lasted a week. By the second week she was back full speed ahead. They couldn't help but respect her determination to get back to normal and her devotion to her job and her patients.

When Chase came out of the elevator, she turned down the hallway where her office was located. The blond stopped dead in her tracks when she saw the tall woman leaning against the wall. Chase didn't have to look into the brown eyes staring her way, she could feel them burning a hole through her. *Just when I think my goddamn life is straightening out after being turned upside down, she shows up to fuck it up again. Back into the blender I go.* At that point she began walking towards the woman standing by her closed office door. Chase lost the battle with herself and made eye contact with Remy. *She's so adorable, just looking at her makes me melt.*

Words weren't spoken as Chase moved around Remy and opened her office door. She waved for Remy to walk inside. Chase shut the door behind herself. They both spoke at the same time.

"What…"

"I'm…"

Remy grinned and Chase smiled shyly as they both apologized.

"Why are you here?" Chase finally got a complete sentence out.

"I... uh... I'm glad you're okay."

"I'm fine." Chase calmed her tone slightly. "Thank you for the flowers you sent me, they were beautiful."

"You're welcome. I..." She nervously moved forward and put her hand on Chase's cheek. "I was worried about you. I wanted to see you, but..." Chase closed her eyes and felt the warmth of the tender touch. "I didn't know what to say to you."

Chase finally pulled her head from the clouds and backed away from Remy's touch. "Well, I'm okay now," she said as she leaned back against her desk and crossed her arms. "Why are you here?" she asked again, against her own will.

"I wanted to see you. I... God, Chase. When I heard you'd had a wreck and were in the hospital, I didn't know what to do. No matter how hard I try, I can't help my feelings for you."

"Well, try harder," Chase said sarcastically. "How's Brian?" she added with a touch of vulgarity and rolled her eyes. That comment hit Remy below the belt. She didn't know what to say or do, it was clear Chase didn't want her around.

"I should go." Remy turned to leave the office. "I..." She closed her eyes and turned back around. When Remy opened her eyes again Chase saw the tears. "Chase... I'm in love with you." Tears fell from her beautiful brown eyes. "I'm sorry." She turned and hurried out of the room, leaving Chase dumbfounded.

When reality finally sank in, Chase closed her jaw

as she sat in the chair behind her desk. The words repeated over and over in her head as her own tears slid down her face. She ran both hands through her hair and sighed heavily. *I hate her. I hate her for doing this to me, I hate her for saying that to me, I hate her, I hate her, I hate her.* She squeezed her eyes closed, then opened them. "I'm so goddamn in love with her, I can't think straight," she whispered to herself and wiped the tears from her eyes.

***

An hour later, Chase finished her paperwork and put a big fat end to her long week. She climbed behind the wheel of her new sports car. Her shaky nerves had nothing to do with driving after her accident. No, they were caused by the scene that played out earlier in her office. Chase grabbed her cell and dialed quickly as she waited for the light to turn green.

"Hey, I was just thinking about you," Frankie said as she answered her phone.

"Really? Was it good?" Chase teased.

"Yeah, wonderful as usual smartass." She was so glad to see her best friend getting back to normal after her scary ordeal.

Chase laughed. "Hey, I was wondering... uh, do you happen to have Veronica Petrovski's number?"

"Yes, why? Are you going to finally take her up on her offer?"

"Maybe. Is she still single?"

"I don't know."

"Hmm... I guess I'll take my chances. You wanna call Ping and Gayle and go out tonight?"

"Sure. Are you calling Ronnie?"

"Yeah, maybe I can get her to go with us. I'll meet you guys around nine at Domingo Flamingo's." It was a local upscale bar slash club that was frequented by the gay community, but a large number of straight men and women went there as well. Eduardo Domingo, the owner, just happened to be the boyfriend of Paul Rainer, the owner of the local coffee shop and deli that the girls went to regularly.

Chapter 10

The bar was crowded by the time Chase arrived with Ronnie at her side. She was surprised when Ronnie said she'd love to go out. Chase picked her up. Ronnie asked about the accident and how she was doing while they were on the way to the bar.

Chase was dressed in jeans and a black spaghetti strap shirt that showed off her tan skin and the lean muscles in her upper body. She was also wearing flip flops. Chase always had on flip flops unless she was working. Ronnie was in jeans as well, with a white halter top and sandals. Her dark curly hair hung past her shoulders, and her olive skin matched her dark eyes perfectly.

"Hey guys!" Chase hugged her friends. "You all remember Ronnie, don't you?"

"Yes. Hey how are you?" Gayle shook her hand and Ping said hey to her as well. Chase was wondering where Maureen was, she actually hadn't seen her since before the accident, but with everything going on she'd completely forgotten to ask.

"Hey! I'm glad you made it." Frankie hugged Ronnie.

"Well, you can thank Chase." Ronnie smiled. Chase went to the bar and ordered a round for the group. They gathered around a small table in the corner. At least thirty people were on the dance floor. Some women were dancing with women, and some with men. Everyone seemed to be having a good time.

Ronnie leaned towards Chase. "Dance with me." A fast song was blaring over the speakers. Chase set her beer down and grabbed Ronnie's hand, leading her to the center of the room. Chase and Ronnie danced with each other until a slower song came on. They stepped closer and continued to sway together. Chase was surprised at how easily she fell into step with Ronnie. Their hands wandered as they wrapped their arms around each other. Ronnie brushed her lips against Chase's. Chase froze at first and then parted her lips to allow the kiss to go further. When their lips parted, Ronnie whispered in Chase's ear, "You're dangerous."

"Why?" Chase asked with a grin.

"You make me come undone," Ronnie said seductively as she kissed her again.

"Ronnie... we... I'm not..." Chase tried to speak.

"I didn't say I wanted to get married, Dr. Leery." Ronnie laughed. They were still wrapped in each other's arms. She leaned close to Chase's ear. "I just want to get naked and sweaty with you." Chase couldn't find her voice. She swallowed past the lump in her throat, thankful for the semi-dark lighting that was hiding the blush on her face. Ronnie pressed her lips to Chase's once more as their tongues teased each other while the DJ started another song.

By the time the music stopped they were breathing heavy from the dancing and make out session. Chase was unaware of her friends watching the entire incident. Chase and Ronnie walked back to the table and finished their drinks and immediately ordered another round from the first waitress who was walking by.

***

After a few more drinks and dances, Chase noticed Yelena heading their way. Gayle rolled her eyes and Ping threatened to smack her. Ronnie looked quizzically at everyone.

"Hey, babe." Yelena walked right between Ronnie and Chase and pressed her lips against Chase's. Chase quickly pulled away.

"Hi, Yelena." Chase raised an eyebrow at her.

"What? You know you miss this." Yelena winked. Her bleach blond hair was just past her shoulders and her fake boobs were popping out of her tied top. The playboy bunny definitely hadn't changed much. Yelena noticed Ronnie giving her the 'who the fuck are you' look. "Chase, baby, introduce me to your friend."

Ugh! She did her best to keep her temper. "This is Veronica Petrovski. Ronnie, this is Yelena Guichard." Yelena grinned and eyed Ronnie up and down, then pressed her lips to Chase's one more time. Again, Chase pulled away.

"I shot a new centerfold. I'll mail you a copy." She winked. "In case you forgot what this looks like." Chase shook her head with disgust. "I should go, it was good to see you again love. Call me sometime, we'll hook up." Yelena walked away in her tight pants.

"Who the hell is she?" Ronnie asked.

The entire group laughed and said at the same time, "French bitch."

"Huh?" Ronnie looked at them curiously.

Chase laughed again. "Yelena's my ex-girlfriend."

"Oh," Ronnie said as her eyebrows went up into her hairline.

"Long story short, she's a model, or more along the lines of a centerfold. Anyway, we were together for a little over two years."

"Hmm."

"Yeah, let's just say I cleaned house one day and tossed the trash to the road."

"She's good looking." Ronnie tried to sound positive.

"Yeah, if you like fake!" Gayle added.

To be honest, Yelena was never Chase's type. She just seemed to fit at the time, almost like Ronnie was doing now. Chase wasn't the sort of person to use someone, but if Ronnie just wanted to have a little fun with no strings attached, why not?

"Come on, let's dance again." Ronnie pulled Chase back to the dance floor. The song was semi-fast, but the next song was slow. Once again, they were in each other's arms swaying to the soft beat.

Ronnie slid her hands into the back of Chase's short hair and pulled her in for another mouthwatering kiss. She playfully bit Chase's lip. Chase parted Ronnie's lips and forced the kiss deeper. Ronnie broke away breathless, she ran her tongue along Chase's ear then whispered. "I figured you'd give in and play eventually."

Chase grinned.

"Let's get out of here," Ronnie said with a wink.

***

Chase ended up at Ronnie's town house since she's

the one that drove them anyway, so she'd need to take Ronnie home eventually. Ronnie wasted no time. Once they were inside, she was all over Chase. Chase was led to the bedroom before she ever had a chance to look around.

"I've wanted to feel you against me since the first day I laid eyes on you," Ronnie said as she pressed her lips to Chase's. Their mouths parted and hands wandered. Chase's entire body fluttered when Ronnie's warm hands slipped under her shirt. The pounding in her ears blocked out any rational thoughts that she was having.

Minutes later both women were rolling around on top of the comforter naked. Chase ran her hands over Ronnie's skin as if she was outside of her own body. Her mind stared into space while she gave only her body to this woman. Sweat ran down both of their bodies as Ronnie pushed Chase back onto the bed and entered her, sliding easily through the wetness. Chase arched her back and closed her eyes. As she began to climax, the darkness behind her eyelids filled with an image of Remy, focusing on her irresistible eyes. Chase's eyes flew open, and she pulled away from the woman who was on top of her. Ronnie sensed the tension and sat up.

"Are you okay?" she asked.

Chase took a couple deep breaths to clear her mind. "Uh... yeah. Yeah, I'm fine. I got a head rush that's all." She smiled apologetically. Ronnie kissed her passionately. Chase took over and pushed Ronnie onto her back, she ran one hand across Ronnie's chest, softly pinching her nipples, then further down her abdomen until she felt the tiny wet patch of hair. Chase teased the layers and then slid two fingers inside of her in one fluid motion. Ronnie moaned and begged Chase to go deeper. Chase obliged with deeper and faster thrusts. She ignored the nails digging into her back, praying they didn't leave marks as Ronnie rode her orgasm to its peak.

Ronnie was breathless and sweaty, and her skin was stuck to Chase's like glue. "Oh my god..." She shook her head and smiled. "You... Dr. Leery... are amazing! I don't know who or what was on your mind, but you were definitely somewhere else," she said as she caught her breath.

Chase wasn't sure what to say to her. "I... I'm sorry... I..."

"No, don't be sorry. That was some of the best sex I've ever had." Ronnie smiled again and ran the back of her hand across Chase's cheek.

Chase grinned back at her. *What the hell do you possibly say to that?*

"Who is she?" Ronnie asked as she looked into Chase's green eyes.

"What?" Chase tried to ignore the question and the sadness behind her own eyes. Ronnie sat next to her at the head of the bed. Both of them were still naked. "I could feel it in your touch, and I can definitely see it in your eyes. There's someone there."

"I..." Chase shrugged. "No one, there's no one. I guess I'm just tired. I should probably go."

"You don't have go, but I understand."

"Thanks. I don't mean to run out on you."

"No, it's fine. I'm tired anyway, you wore me out." Ronnie's face was beaming. Chase got up and redressed piece by piece as she found her clothing.

***

Chase pushed the button to lower the top on the

convertible before she pulled out onto the main road to head south towards her condo. She turned up the song that was playing on the radio. Chase felt free in the open salt air as she drove home singing along to the blaring radio. Speeding was a habit she had, a bad habit to say the least. Still, she was very rarely stopped. The Miami-Dade Police Department had much higher priorities than simple speeders. Chase figured she was safe from the cops, so she cruised on.

Chapter 11

Chase spent all day Sunday trying not to feel sorry for herself. What the hell was there to feel sorry for anyway? So, she had a good time with a woman she barely knew, it sure as hell wasn't the first time, and more than likely wouldn't be the last.

Chase spring cleaned her entire condo. The weather felt like spring, even though it was the end of January and technically the middle of winter. "God bless Miami and it's fucking year-round sweltering heat!" she said to herself, since she was alone. She stopped mopping the kitchen floor long enough to drink a cold beer. The XM satellite stereo was blaring a mixture of 80's and 90's music in the living room.

Chase put the mop away and grabbed another beer. Later, she fired up the vacuum and ran it over the area rug on the Bamboo hardwood floor in the living room. As soon as she was finished with that, she ran the dust mop over the wood floor. She'd already vacuumed the spare room downstairs and mopped the tile in the foyer and the spare bathroom. Since she'd started upstairs, that part of the condo was finished already. This was a good thing because she crashed when she finally sat on the couch to take a break. More than likely, it was because of her lack of sleep.

Lately she couldn't find the energy to argue with herself over the situation with Ronnie or whatever it was. Friends with benefits could be something she could handle. Meaningless good sex was always at the top of any lesbian's list. No mellow drama and no U-Haul could definitely be a good thing. On the other hand, she was dealing with Remy and the damn feelings that just wouldn't go away. Apparently, they were stuck with her, along with Remy's last words, stuck like tree sap to a mosquito's ass.

***

A loud knock on the door woke Chase from a sound sleep. She rolled over and hit the floor with a thud. "Ouch! What the hell?" She couldn't believe she'd fallen asleep, but she was very glad she'd forgotten to put the glass coffee table back after she vacuumed. She would've crashed through it.

The person at the door knocked again. The stereo was still blaring when Chase walked across the condo to answer the door.

"Hey," she said as she pulled the door open. "What's up?" Frankie was standing in the doorway.

"I was in the neighborhood..." She walked in and Chase shut the door. "Michael Jackson?" Frankie looked sideways at her friend and chuckled as she started to sing along to 'Beat it'.

"Don't ask." Chase rolled her eyes and went to go turn the music down.

"Man, I haven't heard that in years. Talk about flash back!"

"Yeah, yeah, yeah," Chase laughed.

"When did you get home?" Frankie took on a more serious note and helped herself to a beer from the refrigerator. Chase took the offered beer from her and went to the couch.

"I love it when you come to my house and serve me like you live here. I'm surprised you didn't tell me to sit down and make myself at home." They both laughed.

"Don't change the subject."

"I'm not." Chase kicked her feet up. "I was home late Friday night, why?"

"Uh huh,"

"What?" Chase raised her eyebrows and glared at her best friend.

"After the scene at the bar, I figured you and Ronnie would at least spend the night together. That's all."

"We had sex," Chase said flatly. Frankie almost poured her beer all over herself.

"Excuse me?"

"That's what you wanted to know wasn't it?"

"Well…"

"There's nothing between us, we had a good time together and that's it. Neither of us is nor was looking for anything else."

"Wow." Frankie ran a hand through her shoulder length auburn hair to brush it off her face. "Are you planning on seeing her again?"

"I don't know. Maybe. We left it open so that we could if we wanted to. You know what I mean?"

"Yeah, friends with benefits." Frankie shook her head and laughed. "You're turning into Gayle."

"Ouch! That was a low blow. I don't sleep with every girl I meet, Frankie!"

"True, but you get what you want. I've seen you turn girls down several times, but I've never seen a girl turn you down."

Chase grinned. "Hmm."

"Either way, I'm glad to see you moving on, especially with a lesbian, a single lesbian."

"What's that supposed to mean?" Chase asked as she finished her beer and got up to get another one.

"I take it Remy Sheridan is history," Frankie said loudly.

Chase returned to the couch with two beers. She took a deep breath. Talking about Remy was not what she had in mind. As a matter of fact, she was doing everything she could to get that woman out of her head. Remy Sheridan was a thorn in her side that twisted every time she heard her name or saw her face. "She told me she's in love with me." Chase's jade green eyes bore a hole in the hardwood floor as she stared between her feet.

"What! Oh my god! When? What did you say to her?" Frankie was hysterical.

"Friday, in my office. I didn't have time to say anything. She started crying and said she was in love with me. Then stormed out."

"Holy shit." Frankie shook her head and drank a few sips of her beer. "You're in love with her too, aren't you?" She didn't have to look at Chase when she didn't say anything, Frankie already knew the answer. "Oh, Chase." Her heart broke for her best friend.

Chase let out a long sigh. "There's nothing I can do about it." She finished her beer and realized she hadn't eaten all day, and by the looks of the number of empty bottles in the trash she'd consumed at least four beers, no wonder her head was starting to spin. "Are you hungry?"

"Yeah,"

"Wanna go to Rainer's?"

"Soup and a sandwich do sound good."

"Actually, that sounds really good," Chase said.

***

Chase and Frankie had just finished their dinner. They continued to sit at their usual corner table in the back of the restaurant. Frankie ordered dessert and Chase decided to help her eat the giant piece of raspberry cheesecake.

"Wow, this is good. I wish Paul would give me his damn recipe," Frankie said between bites. She just happened to notice a tall, short haired brunette woman walk in with an equally tall sandy-haired man. They took a table towards the front of the small restaurant. Chase followed her eyes to see what was so important behind her. As she turned her head, she met Remy's eyes from across the room.

"I'm moving out of South Beach," Chase said in monotone when she turned back towards Frankie.

"I think you were here first," Frankie replied sarcastically. "I can't believe she's still with him. I don't know about you, but I want to smack her upside her head. And she's one of my biggest artists!"

"No one said artists weren't stupid, Frankie. Although, I think she's just confused."

"Don't make excuses for her!" Frankie spoke louder than she meant to. A few people turned their way.

"I'm not. Trust me, that's the last fucking thing I want to do." Chase grabbed the check when the waitress set it down. Frankie tried to snatch it from her, but she was unsuccessful. Chase slipped her Visa into the slot and handed it back to the woman. "Please don't say anything to her, the last thing I need is other people getting involved."

"I know. I just hate to see you get hurt. I'm tired of straight woman trying to break into the lesbian world. All they do is break your heart, then run back to their fucking boyfriends or husbands or whatever they have with a penis."

Chase stood up. "I agree."

"You know I have to stop and speak to them. Unfortunately, I can't let what happened between you two affect my business."

"I know. I can handle it. She can't say anything stupid in front of him anyway." She followed Frankie as they walked towards Remy's table.

"Good evening, Remy, Brian." Frankie shook their hands. "It's good to see you."

"Good to see you too," Brian said. "Hello again, Dr. Leery. How are you?"

"Fine thanks. And you?" She gave him her best 'eat shit' smile, and then glared at Remy.

"Hi, it's nice to see you again." Remy finally coughed out a couple of words, all the while staring eye to eye with Chase.

Chase sucked in a breath. "Likewise." She pretended to smile, as her heart shattered into pieces. She tried not to initiate any further dialogue. Luckily, Frankie redirected the conversation.

"We'll let you guys eat. I just wanted to stop and say hi."

They said a quick goodbye and smiled. Chase wanted to throw up in the bushes when they made it out to the sidewalk. *It's time to be the bigger person here, Leery.*

You can't let yourself get like this every time you see them. You know she's going to be out with him. Goddamn straight women and their fucking experiments! Her pep talk worked for the time being at least.

"Hey, when's the last time you did anything remotely healthy, Frankie?" Chase asked.

"Why? You have that look on your face. The look that I do not like, and you know it." Frankie raised an eyebrow at her best friend as they walked down the sidewalk towards Chase's convertible.

Chase wiggled her eyebrows. This was a bad sign and Frankie knew it. She knew this look very well. "What the hell do you want to do? Isn't it enough that you run on the beach on your days off, if you have any. Now you're dragging me god only knows where, to do god only knows what."

"Oh, calm down! You sound like an old goat!"

Frankie smacked her. "I beg your pardon! I AM NOT OLD!"

Chase simply shrugged and pulled the car out into the traffic. She was headed towards the health club next to her condo complex on the other end of South Beach.

***

An hour later, both women were standing in the middle of the indoor racquetball court covered in sweat. Since Chase had a membership, she kept her equipment in her locker. She happened to have a few extra pairs of shorts and tee shirts and another pair of sneakers that Frankie was able to wear. Chase also had a couple of racquets and pairs of glasses. She always called racquetball her 'release sport', meaning when she needed to let go of some aggression, she'd go smash the little rubber ball against the wall as hard as she possibly could, then get the hell out the way before smacking it again. She usually played alone for that reason. No one in their right mind would enter that room if they wanted to exit alive. She took it easy on Frankie. Although Frankie had played with her many times over the years that they'd been friends, she always knew when not to go play racquetball with Chase.

"I'm surprised you haven't taken my head off by now," Frankie said as she caught her breath.

"You're old, I'm being gentle," Chase chuckled.

"You fucker!" Frankie slammed the ball against the wall behind Chase's head. Chase ducked and spun around to slam it back in the opposite direction.

Both women continued to pound the hell out of the little blue ball on all four walls. Chase could feel the sweat running down the side of her face and between her shoulder blades. Frankie wasn't in as good a shape as Chase, but she was holding her own in the battle of who could hit the ball the hardest and be set up and ready for the next shot. Chase stopped keeping score a long time ago. Instead, she just had fun letting out the built-up steam between her ears with her best friend.

Chapter 12

Monday morning rolled around quickly. Chase had already been through two meetings and was headed into a Mitral Valve Replacement Surgery when her phone rang. Frankie left her a voice mail saying how badly her body hurt from their vigorous workout, and how she demanded a rematch. Chase smiled and made a mental note to call her and jerk her chain later.

***

Almost a month later February was gone, along with Valentine's Day and the minimal amount of cool weather that Miami would see for the rest of the year. Chase was boarding a large plane headed to New York City, where she was going for a Cardiothoracic Conference for a week. Definitely not something she was looking forward to. She felt sorry about missing the 'Spring Art Show' at Deluca's Art Gallery. Surely, Frankie would have a hundred 'you owe me's' ready for her by the time she returned.

After a two-hour layover in Atlanta, her plane arrived on time. The car service was waiting outside for her after she picked up her luggage from the baggage claim area. Minutes later she arrived in the middle of the city in front of the Central Park Hotel. The bell hop, which was dressed like a penguin in a tuxedo, helped get her bag from the driver and ushered her inside. Chase smiled politely and checked into her room. When she finally made it to the tenth floor, she was surprised to see how nice the space was. She tipped the suited guy and shut the door behind him. She could have easily carried her one hanging bag and her wheeled laptop case, but he refused to let her carry her bags, citing it was the hotel's policy to not allow any guest to carry their own luggage. She shrugged and handed him the handle to the heavy hanging bag on wheels. She refused to give up her laptop case though.

After a quick potty break, she put her suit jacket back on and adjusted the collar of her canary yellow blouse. Chase made her way down to the ballroom where the registration booth was located. She didn't realize there would be close to a thousand surgeons at this conference. Most of the ones that she'd attended in the past had no more than four or five hundred.

***

Gayle and Ping walked into Deluca's Art Gallery. Frankie spotted them from across the room and shuffled over to greet her friends. Remy watched from the corner of the room. The distinguished blond was nowhere around.

"Hey, guys! Glad you could make it." Frankie hugged Ping and Gayle.

"Wouldn't miss it!" Gayle smiled. "Although, I'm sure Chase is sorry she's not here."

"Yeah, she's already called me three times today

between her meetings."

"Man, I wouldn't want to be in her shoes. I thought my meetings were boring. Who the hell wants to listen to someone talking and showing pictures of blood and guts for a week?"

"Gross, Ping. I think we get the point!" Gayle shook her head.

Frankie saw Remy keeping a steady eye on the door and watching her friends as they roamed the room looking at various paintings. She was obviously looking for someone. Someone that Frankie knew wouldn't be there. She wormed her way around talking to different artists and potential buyers until she came up to Remy and Brian.

"How are you doing?" Frankie asked Remy.

"Good. I always get so nervous when I'm showing." Brian put his arm around her shoulders compassionately. Frankie saw the slight flinch in Remy's body. A very small, almost miniscule part of her felt sorry for the young woman.

"The jitters never leave some people. You simply just learn how to overcome the pressure and hide the fact that your insides are tied in a knot." She smiled kindly.

"Remy has a habit of staring at the floor when she's nervous. Luckily, she's been able to forget about it," Brian said with a grin as he squeezed the tall woman's shoulders once more and then dropped his arm.

"Yes well, I haven't noticed. Besides, your work is amazing. I already have a list of potentials to call Monday morning."

"That's great." Remy smiled.

"In fact, if you would excuse us for a minute Brian, I'd like to go over a few names on the list with Remy."

"Sure, I'll go check out the competition," He teased

and kissed her cheek before walking away. Remy seemed to ignore the gesture.

Frankie stepped closer to Remy's side and whispered, "She's not coming." Remy stared at the ground and tried to find her voice, but Frankie cut her off. "She's in New York City." Remy lifted her brown eyes shyly to meet Frankie's. Frankie noticed a tall blond with big boobs headed her way. *Who invited her?* She continued her conversation with Remy before the playboy bunny made her way through the crowd.

"I don't know what's going on between you two and honestly it *is* my business. You're one of my biggest clients and she's my best friend. Now is not the time to discuss this, but I think you and I should have a conversation soon." Frankie stepped back. "Before she comes home."

"Hey, Frankie."

"Yelena. How are you?" Frankie shook her hand.

"Good. I heard about the show and decided I'd check it out in hopes that you picked up some talent this year." She smiled sarcastically.

Frankie wanted to tell her she wouldn't know talent if it slapped her across the face. Instead, she smiled and introduced Remy as one of her biggest artists.

"Yes, I believe I've seen her work." She shrugged. She probably would make a good model if she wasn't so fake, but Playboy and Hustler seemed to suit her just fine. "Where's Chase? She never misses a show."

"She's at a conference in New York."

"Oh. Too bad. I was hoping to see her. Do tell her I said hey." She smiled and walked away. Remy looked puzzled. Frankie answered the question before Remy could ask it.

"She's Chase's ex-girlfriend."

"Oh."

***

Chase let a few of the other female doctors talk her into getting a limo and going out on the town for a night in the middle of the week. She donned her best pair of jeans, and a black halter top with black leather ankle boots and a black leather jacket. The other four girls were dressed similarly in jeans, nice tops, and leather boots and jackets.

The white limo drove them to one of the hottest bars in town first. Chase started the evening slow, ordering a light beer.

By Midnight they'd been to two bars and a night club. They were now headed into one of the biggest clubs in town. One that housed a little bit of everything, gay, straight, men, women, black, white, transgender, it didn't matter.

Sahara Centrino, a cardiac surgeon from Chicago with shoulder length black hair and dark eyes, seemed to spend the entire night at Chase's side.

"Wanna dance?" Sahara asked as she took Chase's hand in hers. Chase swore up and down the woman was as straight as an arrow and more than likely drunk.

Damn it! I'm a straight woman magnet. Chase tried to refuse but they were already on the dance floor. The fast song quickly turned slow, and Sahara stepped gently into Chase's arms. Her body was soft and warm against Chase's. Her sweet scent tickled Chase's nose. *Goddamn it! Okay, Leery, you can handle this,* Chase said to herself when Sahara's hands ran up the back of her neck and into her short blond hair as she pressed her face against Chase's cheek. The slow dance began to turn seductive, and Chase had no control over the other woman's actions.

She finally gave in when Sahara's soft lips melted against her own. The kiss was delicate at first. Then, Sahara opened her lips allowing Chase's tongue to probe deeper. Chase wrapped her arms around the slender woman's waist and pulled Sahara tightly against her.

When the slow song ended a faster one began. The two women continued to passionately kiss one another in the center of the dance floor. Chase's phone vibrated in her pocket, scaring the shit out of her. She jumped and pushed Sahara away from her as she apologized and took off towards the door.

"This is Dr. Leery." She answered without looking at the caller ID, hoping she caught the call before it went to her voicemail.

"Hey, Chase, it's me." Frankie tried to talk over the background noise. It was obvious Chase was in a bar or a club.

"Oh hey, hold on a second." Chase walked a little way down the sidewalk so she could hear. "Okay, sorry."

"Where are you?"

"Some big nightclub, I'm not sure of the name. A few of the girls in my meeting group wanted to go out, so I decided to tag along. Boy, am I glad you called. How was the show?"

"Good. What's wrong? You sound funny."

"Uh…" Chase shook her head. "One of those girls… let me rephrase that, one of those straight girls was all over me on the dance floor. We were practically about to fuck in front of everyone. Your call stopped me."

"Holy shit."

"I'm glad you called. Sleeping with some strange straight girl is not what I need right now."

"Yeah well, it probably beat running into your nemesis tonight," Frankie said with sarcasm.

"Really,"

"Yeah, the show was great. I'll be swamped next week. But it was obvious that one tall, short haired brunette was moping around like a lost puppy watching the door as if it was going to swallow her whole."

"That bad huh?"

"Oh yeah. So bad in fact, I had to go tell her you weren't coming because you were out of town. I figured her tag along would catch on if I didn't get her refocused."

"Wow. What did she say?"

"Nothing, she looked scared to death. She's so damn shy. It's funny, when we're alone and she's talking about art you can't shut her up. But, as soon as the conversation changes, she seems lost."

"Yeah, she doesn't talk much around me either unless we're alone. Even then, she's pretty quiet, but I haven't actually given her much time or room to talk," Chase said with a hint of a smile that she quickly wiped off.

"I told her we needed to talk before you came home."

"Oh, Frankie, you're going to scare the girl to death."

"I'm sick of the cat and mouse game, Chase. It's very evident that she's in love with you, and you're doing a damn good job of hiding your feelings from everyone but me. She's hurt you enough and now it's affecting my business. You're my best friend. What happens when you decide not to come to the gallery anymore because she's there?"

"Frankie, we've been best friends for years. Do you honestly think I'll stop going to the shows because of a woman? I love art, and I love going to the shows. No matter what happens or doesn't happen between me and Remy, I'll still go to her shows and still buy her paintings if I like them."

Frankie laughed. "You're too rational for your own good, Chase Leery."

"Thank you. Whoa! Hey... hey!" Chase waved her arms and whistled.

"What the hell!" Frankie yelled.

"Hold on a second." Chase moved the phone away and slid into the taxi and told the driver the name of her hotel. 'Okay, sorry I was flagging down a cab. My bar hopping night is over."

"I'm sorry. I'll let you go so you can go back inside."

"No way, I would've probably taken that woman back to my room. I hope I don't run into her tomorrow."

"Yikes."

"No kidding. I'm so not looking for a one-night stand, especially with a straight woman. Ugh!" Chase threw her head against the back seat of the cab.

"I forgot to mention French bitch showed up tonight."

"She did not!" Chase sat up straight.

"Damn sure did. When I was talking to Remy actually."

"Did you introduce them?"

"Yes. As soon as she was gone, I told Remy who she was."

"Oh god. Well, I doubt she'll want to talk to me anyway now."

Frankie laughed. "I doubt it. Go get some sleep. I'll see you in a couple of days."

***

Chase was glad to be back in Miami. Five days of lectures and presentations, including one she had presented herself, was enough to make the dead roll over. She was tired and cold. Her little silver convertible Mercedes was a sight for sore eyes.

A half hour later, Chase pulled up to her condo. She wanted to kiss the tile in the foyer when she walked in. "It's wonderful to be home." She put her suitcase upstairs in her room and changed into shorts and a tee shirt before opening all the blinds to let the sunlight in.

As soon as Chase sat on the couch to relax with a cold beer, her cell phone rang. "Goddamn it, I'm home for an hour and someone's already dying to talk to me." She grabbed the phone and didn't recognize the number.

"This is Dr. Leery."

"Hi." The quiet voice was barely audible.

"Remy?"

"Yeah,"

"What... uh.... hi." Chase wasn't sure what to say.

"I know you're probably still out of town..."

"No, I got back a little while ago. Are you okay?" She didn't like the tone in the quiet voice on the other end of the line.

"Yeah, can we talk?"

"Uh... sure. Yeah."

"Can I come over?" Remy asked.

"Where's... uh..." Chase kicked herself for constantly forgetting the man's name. She never forgot someone's name, but for some reason she could care less what his name was.

"Brian. He's leaving for a lunch meeting."
"All right. I'll be here."

Chapter 13

Chase was asleep on the couch when the doorbell rang. She noticed Pulp Fiction was playing on the TV on the wall when she got up to answer the door. *Damn, I love that movie. The only time I get to see it is when it's half over. Note to self: buy the DVD!* She pulled the door open. Remy was standing there in thin jogging pants, and a tank top. Chase fought off the urge to pull the woman into her arms when she looked into eyes staring back at her, full of desire.

"Come in." She stepped away from the door. Remy walked through the foyer and Chase shut the door. Remy turned back towards her, and their lips met softly. Remy ran her hands through Chase's short hair and Chase pulled the taller woman as tightly against her as she could, running her hands across the soft skin under her tank top.

Chase parted her lips, Remy tasted further until their tongues touched. They filled each other with the deep passion that burned between them. They made it as far as the couch. Remy laid back and Chase crawled on top of her. She slowly pulled Remy's tank top over her head and tossed it to the floor. Their lips were fused together as they kissed once more. Chase broke the kiss and ran her lips and tongue down Remy's neck and across her chest, before placing light kisses all over Remy's soft stomach as she slid her pants down.

Minutes later all their clothes were in various piles on the living room floor. Remy pinned Chase down to the couch and kissed every inch of the blonde's body that she could reach, going very slowly over her breasts to tease them. She let go with one hand so she could slide it between Chase's legs. Chase raised her hips urging Remy to go inside of her. Her mind was searching, and her body was begging for release. Remy gave in and entered Chase, feeling the wetness fill her hand when she teasingly pulled her fingers back out. Chase gasped and grabbed a handful of Remy's short brown hair with her free hand. Remy straddled Chase's thigh and slid against it hard enough for her folds to open and cover the path with warm moisture.

"You feel that?" Remy said with a breathless whisper. Chase nodded. Her entire body was on fire, threatening to explode on its own any minute. "You do that to me. God, Chase. I can't stop thinking about you, the way you feel against me, wanting you inside of me, longing to be inside of you, dying to taste you…" Remy leaned down and kissed Chase's soft pink lips. Their kiss easily turned forceful as the intense fire burned between them. Each woman pled her case to other through hunger filled, passionate caresses.

They were oblivious to the fact that they were squished together on the couch when there was a very comfortable king-sized bed upstairs. They continued to kiss and enter each other, riding to new heights as their orgasms peaked simultaneously. Chase threw her head back and pulled Remy against her.

They fell asleep listening to each other's heartbeat and shallow breaths.

***

An hour later Chase awoke to the sound of the doorbell. Images of their lovemaking flashed through her mind when Remy stirred against her. Reality slapped her in the face when she heard a loud pounding on the door followed by a man's voice. *Oh shit!*

Remy dove off the couch and rushed around trying to put her clothes back on correctly. Chase was right behind her, straightening the last of her clothing as she pulled the door open. Brian was standing in the doorway. *Shit, Shit, Shit!*

"Oh. Hi, Dr. Leery. Sorry to bother you. I'm looking for Remy. I noticed her car outside." Chase wondered how he figured out what condo she was in. Either he was outside watching her, he knocked on every door, or he was tracking her. Before she could answer him, Remy pushed past her.

"I'm right here, Brian," she said sarcastically.

"I was looking all over for you. What are you doing here?" He sounded fairly calm. Maybe he had no idea what had gone on an hour ago.

"I stopped by to see Chase. It's not a big deal. She's purchased one of my paintings."

"Well, we need to talk. Let's go." She hesitated, and then followed him outside. She turned back long enough for Chase to see the sadness in her beautiful eyes.

***

Chase hit the speed dial button on her cell phone as

soon as she shut the front door. She waited for the voice to answer on the other end.

Hey stranger."

"Don't start, Frankie. I'm having a goddamn melt down!"

"What! What's wrong?"

"What the fuck isn't wrong?"

"Huh? I hate it when you talk in riddles, Chase."

"How about Remy came over, we made love, then her boyfriend shows up at my door. I'm not sure if he knew or not. He seemed a little irritated that she was here."

"Back the fucking turnip truck up! You slept with her, AGAIN!" Her voice went up a few octaves on the last word.

"Yes," Chase said under her breath.

"Chase!" Frankie shook her head. "How did he know where she was?"

"I guess he followed her, I don't know."

"Hmm... how did he know which door was yours?"

"Frankie, I don't know. Actually, he looked kind of shocked when I opened the door. I think he either saw her go to this one or knocked on all of them. Maybe he's tracking her phone or something. Honestly, I think he thought she was with another guy. He looked really surprised."

"Holy shit! What did you say to him?"

"What the fuck was I supposed to say? 'Oh hi, I just finished screwing your girlfriend. She'll be out in a minute.'" Chase said with sarcasm. "I said hi, and he said he was looking for Remy. By that time, she pushed past me and spoke to him. They left right after that."

"Wow." Frankie let out a long sigh. "I'm sorry, honey."

"Don't sweat it, it's over now. I guess I'm lucky he didn't knock me out or something."

"No shit! I would've pissed my pants!"

Chase laughed. "I would like to have seen that. And for the record, I was scared to death, but I didn't let him know it. I acted like she stopped by to say hi."

Chapter 14

A month passed. Chase hadn't heard from or seen Remy since that afternoon at her condo. She was worried about her and hoped she was okay. But what went on between Remy and Brian was none of her business, in fact, she was furious with herself for letting things go as far as they had. Frankie, Gayle and Ping did everything they could to keep her mind off of Remy and the incidents that linked them together.

***

Chase donned her cap and surgical mask. Then, she finished scrubbing her arms and hands before entering the surgical suite. The surgery tech met her at the door and assisted her with her sterile surgical gown and gloves. She was glad to see Dr. Henry Grainger in the room already gowned and gloved. She had completely forgotten he was her assistant for this surgery. In fact, she hadn't worked with him since the fatal surgery last year that he assisted her with. Every now and then Chase thought about that day, partly because it started off as the most perfect day of her life and ended as the most tragic. She knew deep down she'd never forget that man or his family, just as she still hadn't forgotten about all her other patients that had died.

The blond said a tiny prayer and smiled at Henry when he joined her next to the patient.

"Morning, Dr. Leery." The black man smiled and began preparing the surgical tools.

"So far so good, Doctor Grainger." The anesthesiologist looked up and nodded as Chase began to open the woman's chest to perform the Mitral Valve Replacement. At this point in her career, Chase had completed so many of these procedures she could probably do this one with her eyes closed. But she still followed every precaution, taking her time and using her own established technique.

Two and a half hours later, the operation was completed, and the woman was sent to recovery with no problems. Chase spoke to her family as soon as she cleaned up, then made her way back to her own office to go over her schedule for the following week since it was already Friday.

***

Chase finished her paperwork and was about to answer the page she'd just received when she heard a soft knock on her door.

"Come in." She called out and hung up the telephone. When the door opened, Remy's tall slender frame was standing there with her gorgeous brown eyes gazing down at the blond behind the desk in dark blue scrubs. Chase wished God would turn her into Smurf size so she wouldn't be seen by the woman, but it was too late.

"Hi," Remy said as she shut the door.

"What brings you here?" Chase said loosely.

"I... we need to talk..."

"We tried that last time we were together, remember?"

A faint smile crossed Remy's face, and then faded away. "I..."

Chase took a deep breath. "What are we supposed to say to each other, Remy?"

"I don't know." The brunette tried to speak. "I'm so confused."

"You're confused?!" Chase tried not to let the tone in her voice rise. "I don't know whether I'm coming or going anymore, Remy. All I think about is you. I try so fucking hard to get over you and as soon as I think I'll make it to the other side, you appear, and my entire world falls apart again."

"I don't know what to do, Chase. I... you're the only woman I've ever been with." She ran a hand through her short brown hair. "You're the only person that has ever made me feel like this. I want you so badly I can't see straight. Yet, I'm scared to death. I'm not... well at least I never thought I was... a lesbian." She finished close to a whisper.

"What is that supposed to mean, Remy? Are you still with him?"

"Yes and no. Hell, I don't know anymore." Tears started to slowly roll down her cheeks.

"Look at me." Remy stopped staring at the floor long enough to see the green eyes sparkling in front of her. "I don't want to be your little secret... I can't." Chase let out a long sigh.

"What *do* you want?"

"You, Remy. I want you, and I can't handle having only a part of you, and only when it's convenient."

"What if I can't give you that?" Remy broke their gaze, but quickly moved her eyes back to Chase's.

"Then we should just be friends," Chase said with as much courage as she could muster up. Remy squeezed her eyes closed. When she opened them, the tears started to flow. She left the room before Chase could stop her. Chase wiped away her own tears and wished she could take the words back. *Maybe this is best. Maybe... maybe my ass.* She ran both hands through her hair, drew in a deep breath, and then slowly let it out ending with a long sigh.

***

Three weeks later Chase was back to working a hundred hours a week. She refused to feel sorry for herself or let the situation bother her any longer. Damn it, she was bound and determined to get over Remy Sheridan.

Gayle called Chase and invited her to go out with Gayle and her new 'flavor of the month' Victoria. Ping was also going, at least that would give Chase someone to talk to while Gayle did her usual petting all over the new woman she was with. So, Chase agreed to go. Since Frankie was working late, she wasn't going.

***

Chase was two stiff double Jack on the rocks into the night when Gayle bumped her arm and leaned over.

"Look over there in the corner," she whispered.

"What?" Chase glanced around the room. She had no idea what the hell Gayle was talking about. Victoria was walking towards them. Chase couldn't help eyeing the pretty young girl Gayle was seeing. She was about Chase's height with long blond hair and blue eyes. Chase figured the girl to be maybe twenty-five. Gayle saw who Chase was looking at.

"Not her." She smacked her arm and pointed. "Over there!" Chase followed Gayle's arm. The dance floor opened enough for her to see the other side of the large room. The woman sitting at the table had her back to them. Even in the darkness Chase could make out the figure.

"Goddamn it!" Chase turned back to the bar and ordered another round. The soft hands that thread around her waist and the warm breath on her neck sent goose bumps over her body. Her blood boiled and her libido flew into overdrive.

"Get off of me, Remy," she said through clenched teeth.

"Who's Remy?" The person holding her from behind answered as she pressed her lips to the back of Chase's neck close to her hairline. Chase spun around, nearly knocking the woman over.

"Ronnie!" Chase had the 'deer in the headlights' look on her face. She was expecting Remy behind her, especially after she'd spotted the woman sitting across the bar.

"So, that's her name." Ronnie grinned.

Shit. Son of a bitch! Chase tried to cover it up. "Hey, what are you doing here?"

Ronnie smiled. "I was working on a project with Frankie. She said you were here. She came in with me, but I'm not sure where she went."

"Hmm... she said she wasn't going out."

"I guess I'm pretty good at persuasion."

I'd say so, Chase thought. *This is* not *what I need tonight.* Ronnie ordered herself a drink while Gayle introduced her new 'flame' to Ronnie. Ping was busy flirting with the girl next to her that had just stepped off the dance floor.

"So, what does she look like?" Ronnie asked as she sipped her martini. Her curly black hair hung loosely around her shoulders.

"Who?" Chase asked with a raised eyebrow. *All She Wants To Do Is Dance* started playing on the speakers. Gayle grabbed Chase and took off to the dance floor. The two of them always liked to dance to that song. They could make any woman's head turn just to watch the way they handled each other.

Gayle wrapped her arms around Chase and pressed herself tightly against her, then released her for a turn. They went right back into each other's arms. Chase turned around to let Gayle hold her from behind. They mimicked each other's every move as Chase turned back to face her. They made a fast dance to a fast song look very, very sexual. A few of the women clapped, some whistled. Gayle and Chase just grinned from ear to ear and continued twirling and grinding with each other. When the song ended, they made their way back to the bar. Frankie was laughing and shaking her head. Victoria was ready to slap Gayle and Ronnie smiled. She'd seen them dance together before. Ping was off in her own little world, still trying to pick up the girl sitting next to her.

"You two looked good together. But watch this," Ronnie said as she grabbed Chase's hand and led her to the dance floor. Chase smiled when she recognized the song, *Son of a Preacher Man.*

Ronnie threw her arms around Chase's neck and ran

her hands into Chase's hair as they swayed together. Chase released Ronnie's hold long enough to spin her around then catch her and pull her back into her arms. They continued to twirl and grind together until the song was over.

Chase was panting when she made it back to the bar. She quickly drank down the rest of her double Jack and wiped the sweat from her face.

"I think the ladies are lining up to dance with you," Frankie said as she walked up behind Chase and threw her arm around the blonde's shoulders.

"Ha! Not likely. I thought you weren't coming out tonight?"

She shrugged. "I decided I needed a drink. Besides, I'm glad I did. You need someone protecting you with a stick."

Chase shook her head and laughed.

"Hey, love. Where's my dance?" Chase didn't have to turn around; she knew the voice and smelled the familiar perfume. Yelena smacked Chase's butt.

"What brings you out tonight? No sleazy magazine shoots this weekend?"

Yelena smiled. Chase noticed the 'French bitch' was wearing tight jeans and a very low-cut spaghetti strap shirt with a built-in bra that didn't help. Her fake boobs were overflowing. Her wavy, bleach blond hair hung halfway down her back and her hazel eyes glistened in the dark. If she wasn't so fake, Yelena would be a really pretty woman. *Oh well,* Chase thought to herself.

"I remember when we used to get the crowd going on the dance floor. You were always a sexy dancer, love." Yelena winked at Chase.

"She still is," Ronnie butted in. Yelena raised an eyebrow at her and grinned.

"Did you get the present I sent you?" Yelena was referring to the latest issue of Hustler Magazine where she was the completely nude centerfold. Of course, Chase got it. As a matter of fact, she had flipped through it and saw the raunchy pictures of the woman she shared her bed and life with for over two years. She felt disgusted as she tossed it in the trash can.

"Uh… yeah I got it." Chase rolled her eyes.

"So?" Yelena ran her hand through her long hair to push it off her face. "What did you think?"

I think it's trashy, tasteless, trampy… "It's definitely you," she said with sarcasm. Chase still couldn't believe what she ever saw in this woman.

"I'm glad you liked it."

The DJ changed the music to *Wild Thing*. Yelena grabbed Chase's hand and winked. "For old times' sake?" Chase shrugged and followed her to the dance floor.

Yelena stopped in the center of the room, threw her arms around Chase's neck, and rubbed herself all over her. She looked like a stripper dancing on a pole.

Frankie, Ronnie, Gayle, and Victoria watched from the bar.

"Wow. She definitely has some moves," Victoria said. Gayle shot her a look.

"She's so trampy," Frankie added.

"How long were they together?" Ronnie asked as she ordered another drink.

"Uh… a little over two years I think." Frankie sipped her martini. Ping noticed the action on the dance floor.

"What the fuck?!" Ping yelled. "Oh, she is NOT getting her whore claws back into Chase! Frankie, why didn't you stop her?"

"Ping, Chase is an adult, I'm not her keeper." Frankie pushed her auburn hair back behind her ear and out of her face. "She's fine. I seriously doubt Chase will ever mess with her again."

Just then the song was over, and Chase peeled herself away from Yelena and walked back over to her friends.

"What the fuck, Chase?" Ping looked pissed. Chase laughed.

"Calm down, Ping Pong. I'm glad to see you're joining the group though." Chase finished the drink that she'd left at the bar. Gayle leaned over to her.

"She's still here."

"Does it look like I care? I told you it's over."

"I don't think it is."

"Why?"

"Because she's coming this way." Gayle backed up to let Remy get close to Chase. Remy grabbed Chase's hand and their eyes locked. Chase followed the taller woman to the dance floor and completely ignored the questions coming from her friends. When they stopped in the center, Remy thread her arms around Chase's waist and under the back of her shirt, resting her hands against her bare skin. Chase ran her fingers through Remy's short hair. Their bodies fused perfectly together as they swayed to the slow song. Chase's eyes never left the chocolate brown one's staring back at her. Remy ran her hands up and down, caressing Chase's back. Their lips were inches apart, gradually moving closer until they finally met softly. They kissed each other tenderly, never faltering from the dance they shared. They looked like two lovers gently making love on the dance floor.

When the song was over, Chase walked all the way

out of the bar and never turned back when she hit the thick humid air outside. Remy ran after her.

Chapter 15

"Remy. Remy Sheridan!" Ronnie said quizzically. It finally hit her. "Her! I never would've guessed."

"What are you talking about?" Gayle asked.

"Poor, Chase. That bitch has a lot of nerve. She had better never run into me alone; I'll kick her ass." Ping was about to head outside to rescue her friend.

"Calm down guys, Chase is an adult, she can handle herself."

"Chase is in love with her." Ronnie tossed back the last of her drink and set the glass on the bar.

"They're in love with each other," Frankie stated. "Honestly, I hope they work it out one day."

"Yeah, me too. Chase looks so sad all the time, except when she's with her. I've never seen chemistry like that. Did you see them dancing?" Gayle shook her head.

"I've never seen two people more in love. How long has this been going on?" Ronnie asked Frankie.

"Um… god, probably six or eight months."

"Holy shit. Wait, isn't Remy… I mean she has…"

"A boyfriend… we know and so does Chase."

Ronnie shrugged. "Talk about cluster fuck."

"Yeah, no kidding," Gayle added.

***

Remy caught up with Chase a few blocks away. She grabbed her shirt and spun the smaller woman around. Both women had tears in their eyes.

"What are you doing to me?" Remy's voice was just above a whisper.

"Me!" Chase yelled as she glared into Remy's eyes. "What the fuck are you doing to me, Remy? Why were you there?"

Remy broke the intense gaze. "I… Brian's out of town at a business meeting, and I guess I wanted to get out of the house. I didn't think you'd be there… I mean… I know a lot of different people go there…"

"What do you want from me, Remy?" Chase sighed.

"You. I'm…" Remy looked into her eyes once more. Chase cut her off.

"We've been down this road. I'm not… this WON'T happen again. Please stay away from me, Remy. I… I can't do this." Chase let tears fall when she turned her back to Remy and walked towards her car.

Minutes later, Remy watched the silver Mercedes sports car drive off. She stood on the sidewalk and cried until there were no tears left to cry.

***

Chase made herself a glass of Jack Daniels on the rocks and walked out onto her balcony. The night was clear, and the sky was full of stars. The ocean waves crashed against the shore over and over in perfect rhythm. Chase didn't feel the cool chill on her skin from wearing only shorts and a small tank top, nor did she feel the wet tears rolling down her cheeks. She grabbed her cell phone a hundred times. She even punched the number in a few times, but never hit send.

"Why? Why her? Why me? Why all of this? Goddamn it I don't understand," She yelled into the moonlight. *I love her so much.* "Please just help me let her go. Help me forget." She sloshed the gold liquid around in her glass and took a long sip. "I... I don't understand why I love her so much... I can't have her. Why did you do this to me? Why!" She hesitated, waiting to hear an answer. Maybe a bum passing by in the sand or a nosey neighbor would say something. Anything, anyone with some kind of rational explanation for the fucked-up situation she was bound and determined to be stuck in for what seemed like forever.

Chase went back through the French doors and set her glass down. She didn't bother changing clothes or even putting flip flops on. She took off through the front door, into the elevator, then out the back entrance of the condo building towards the ocean. She ran right into the saltwater and dove headfirst.

She yelped when she popped up fifteen or twenty feet away soaked to the bone treading water. For March, the water was still rather cold; she figured probably around sixty-five degrees. She swam for a few more minutes before going back to her condo upstairs.

Chase was sober by the time she walked into her condo. She hadn't even bothered to lock the door, much less take her key with her. She quickly stripped her cold, wet, clothes off and tossed them in the laundry basket. She was freezing and sticky from the saltwater. She took a hot shower and let the dual stream massage the tense muscles in her back and shoulders.

***

Frankie stood at Chase's door banging profusely. The sleeping blond finally pulled it open.

"You look like shit," Frankie said as she pushed past her with two steaming cups of coffee from Rainer's.

"Gee thanks. I was going for the hung over, brokenhearted, everyone rains on my fucking parade look. I'm glad you like it because it's becoming a permanent fixture in my wardrobe," Chase said sarcastically as she snatched the coffee and shut the door. She walked right past her auburn-haired best friend and sat on the couch with her feet up on the table. She was thankful she wasn't scheduled for a shift at the hospital today, although she was always on call for emergencies. It was nice to have a Saturday off and since she'd worked the past ten days with no day off, she was planning on sleeping the entire day until her best friend practically beat the door down at nine a.m.

"What happened when you two left last night? Neither of you came back inside."

"I don't feel like talking about it." Chase turned the TV on and stared at a rerun of 'The Golden Girls'. "I told her to stay away from me," she finally said with a long sigh, her head pounded, and her heart ached. *I think I'd rather have a heart attack, I bet it hurts less.*

Frankie wanted to kick Remy's ass for the pain in her friend's eyes, but to be truthful they both had a part in it. Still, she felt bad for Chase and hated to see her so sad. When things went sour with Yelena, she never saw the same hurt in Chase's normally vibrant green eyes. Now, they were dark epitomes of her soul, open and vulnerable.

Ironically, Chase wished it was already night out so she could go drink in the corner of some rundown hole-in-the-wall bar. At that rate she'd become a drunk quicker than she could blink her eyes. Drinking wasn't the answer to anything, but damn it she wanted a drink, and she just woke up. This was not a good sign.

"Vacation..." That was all she heard of the one-sided conversation Frankie was having.

"Huh?" Chase questioned with a sideways glance.

"Damnit, woman, did you not hear anything I just said?" Frankie shook her head. "You're stressed out, and I think it would do you some good to take a small vacation."

"Nah, running from life doesn't do anything but make it worse when it catches up to you. I made this mess and now I need to clean it up."

"Somehow I don't think it'll be that simple, honey." Frankie's heart was broken for Chase and everything she was going through. She wished deep down that Remy would wake up and leave her boyfriend to make a life with Chase. If one thing was for sure, Remy would be loved unconditionally for the rest of her life. Chase adored her to the depths of her soul. Frankie couldn't even think of a time when she'd loved someone that much in her entire life.

Chase let the warm tears fall. "It has to be, Frankie. This is killing me and if I don't stop the bleeding, I'll die." Frankie put her arm around Chase's shoulders and Chase leaned into the curve of her shoulder.

"I could smack that woman! I'm sorry you're hurting, honey. I'd tell you it'll get better and trust me it will, eventually, but I know that's not what you want to hear right now. I honestly don't know what to say to you. Straight women are the worst women to get involved with.

They will break your heart and their own and keep on going like it was nothing."

Chase sniffled. "Their bite is much larger than their bark. How could I be so stupid, Frankie?"

"You're not stupid, Chase. A little gullible when it comes to women maybe, but not stupid." Frankie gave her a hearty grin and a light squeeze.

"I wish I could go to sleep and wake up when this is all over. Unfortunately, I have to suck it up and act like an adult."

"Are you off today?"

"Yeah, I'm on call as usual, but I'm not on rotation this weekend."

"It's about fucking time. You damn sure put in enough hours at that hospital."

"Yeah, I'm actually going to San Diego Monday for a National Heart Surgery Convention. Oh, what fun," she said sarcastically.

"Goodie!" Frankie laughed. "It'll be good for you to get away. How long will you be gone?"

"A week,"

"Hmm… hey, you wanna go with me to West Palm? I want to check out the new artist in Jon Paul's Gallery," Frankie said.

"I guess a road trip isn't out of the question." Chase sat up and turned back to face Frankie. "I need to shower. What time do you want to leave?"

"As soon as you're ready, I'll wait for you."

Chapter 16

"I'm glad I decided to come with you," Chase said as she stared at the Atlantic Ocean from the window of Frankie's Lexus. "I needed a break, that woman wears me out," she sighed. They were barely ten minutes into their hour and a half drive.

"The CD case is behind your seat. Pick us out something good. I'm tired of seeing you in this depressed miserable state of I-don't-give-a-shit. Honestly, it's starting to rub off," Frankie said through a smile. Chase ignored the comment. She knew she wasn't good company lately, but what was she supposed to do? Act like everything was peachy keen. She reached behind the seat and flipped through the hard case. She giggled at some of the old CD titles and gasped at others. Frankie had a small collection ranging from rock bands of the 80's to classical, including various hip hop and country selections as well. Truthfully, Chase would rather ride in silence, but all that did was let her mind wonder over thoughts of Remy and she did not want her weekend once again ruined by that woman. She chose a CD titled Various Hair Bands of the 80's.

Frankie raised her eyebrows and looked at Chase

with surprise when she heard *Sweet Cherry Pie* start playing on the radio.

"What? Maybe I wanted a pick-me-up." Chase wiggled her eyebrows as she sang along loudly. "God, I haven't heard this in years!" She smiled. Frankie couldn't believe she actually remembered the words to the song. She couldn't help joining in the singing.

Minutes later, *Once Bitten Twice Shy* began playing and Chase turned the radio even louder. "Holy shit, do you remember me singing this at karaoke in *Bahama Mama's* in the Keys?"

Frankie's face lit up. "Oh my god! That was forever ago." Both women sang along to the song, surprisingly on key. Frankie played air drums on the steering wheel and Chase played air guitar and air piano on the dash. Passersby looked at them like they were nuts, but neither woman took notice as they cruised down the interstate.

"We should definitely plan a trip back to the Keys," Frankie said when the song ended.

"That would great, but I'm so busy with the hospital right now, I don't know when I could go." Chase felt the tension creep back into her face.

"We'll figure something out, that damn place owes you some much needed vacation time." Frankie grabbed her best friend's hand and squeezed it. Chase slowly smiled once again. The last thing Frankie wanted was to see those sad puppy dog eyes again. She brought her friend along to cheer her up and she had been doing a good job until Chase was reminded of home. Before either of them could change the song, *I Hate Myself for Loving You* began playing. Chase couldn't react fast enough, her entire body stiffened up and she blinked back at the tears. Frankie finally managed to change the song, but it was too late. She wanted to slap the hell out of Remy Sheridan for being so cowardice towards Chase's feelings and her own personal actions. Why couldn't she leave her alone? Why couldn't they leave each other alone for that matter? Chase had always been one of the strongest and most down-to-Earth people that Frankie had ever met. That's probably why they were such good friends.

The next song quickly began. As soon as Frankie recognized the words to *Edge of a Broken Heart* she snatched the CD out of the radio and tossed it out the window. Chase looked over at her in amazement with large eyes and raised eyebrows. They stared at each other for a second, and then both women busted out laughing hysterically. Chase was laughing so hard she had tears streaming down her face. She was crying from the laughter, but also about the feelings that both songs had dragged to the surface. Frankie was practically swerving on the road because she was hysterical. Neither woman could speak, they laughed close to ten minutes non-stop.

***

Chase sat in a small beachside bar sipping a Margarita and watching the young women walk by in bikinis. She and Frankie spent two hours cruising through the gallery examining different pieces, mostly by the new artist Jon Paul contracted a few months back. He had an abstract style of various colors and brush strokes. Chase found it interesting, but it didn't compare to the abstract artists that Frankie had in her gallery.

"You know he came to me first," Frankie said as she sipped her Mai Tai. "I turned him down. I didn't really have the room at the time anyway. It's not that he's bad, I just didn't think I could get his work to move. Jon says he's had a handful of sales, but nothing to shake a stick at. Personally, I wouldn't mind owning a piece or two; some of them had unbelievable color contrasts."

"I like his work better than those damn Monet's." Chase rolled her eyes. In the back of her mind, she thought about the painting hanging in her living room. The first painting of Remy Sheridan's to ever be sold out of the Deluca Gallery.

"Have you seen the value of those paintings that you hate so much?" Frankie asked.

"Nope, I let that stupid bimbo spend a ton on each one though." Chase shook her head and finished her drink, signaling the waiter to bring her another. "My parents would freak if they knew I spent that kind of money on two things that hang on a damn wall."

"She got a hell of a deal on them though. One thing that woman could do was shop."

"I second that." They both laughed.

"Seriously, what are you going to do with them?" Frankie asked.

"Considering French bitch spent a good chunk of my savings on those damn things that I don't care for, I should probably sell them."

"Maybe she heard of your parents hitting the Lottery ten years ago. Hell, that's probably how she found you; her grave digging ass," Frankie squawked. Chase's parents had won fifteen million dollars in the state lottery ten years before and decided on a lump settlement. They took half of it for themselves and put the other half in a trust fund for Chase. She used some to buy her condo and pay for med-school, but other than that, she never spent any of it. Her car and other various luxuries were purchased from her work paychecks.

"You're probably right, who knows." Chase thanked the waiter and took a long swallow of the sour drink. "Let's put them in your gallery."

"Are you nuts?" Frankie almost fell out of her chair.

"What?" Frankie shot her a sideways glance.

"I am not putting those on display anywhere near my gallery. Do you know how many people will pay money just to come see the damn things? Hell no. Ugh uh!" Frankie was shaking her head as she spoke.

"Okay, what's the best thing to do?"

"I'll broker them out for you at an internet private auction. We'll show your original documents but keep the paintings on your wall until they sell. I know they're copies, but they were done by a very prominent artist and are in high demand."

"That's fine. I don't care as long as they're gone. They make me feel snooty when people find out about them. I don't like flaunting my money." Chase sipped her drink and took the time to observe the tall blond walking by in a red string bikini. "Personally, not to bring her up, but I'd rather see Remy's work on my walls."

Frankie saw the smile tug at Chase's lips at the mention of Remy's name, it disappeared just as quickly. "Her work is definitely incredible, full of passion."

"Everything about her is full of passion." Chase's voice was barely above a whisper. Frankie took that as a cue to change the subject.

"What time did you want to head back?"

"Whenever you're ready."

Chapter 17

Chase sat in the First-Class cabin of the large plane as it flew over the Grand Canyon. They were high above the clouds so she couldn't see much when she gazed out the window, but the Pilot had announced their position anyway. Chase tried to lay her head back and get some much-needed rest, but flying always made her too wired to sleep. She pulled her briefcase from under the seat in front of her and retrieved the latest copy of Cardiology News before sliding the briefcase back under the seat.

After paying a ridiculous fee plus a tip to the cab driver, Chase walked into the Marriot and checked into her suite. The entire conference was scheduled to start the next morning so she checked-in with the conference group, then went to her room to drop her luggage off. She was in dire need of a drink and the hotel bar seemed decent enough. Minutes later, Chase strolled into the bar dressed in black slacks and a short sleeved burgundy blouse. She'd left the jacket to her pantsuit in her room. The space was dimly lit, and a large grand piano sat in the corner with an older man in a tuxedo playing an unfamiliar tune.

"What can I get you, Ma'am?" the tall gray-haired

woman behind the bar asked with a hint of a smiled as her eyes passed over Chase not once but twice.

"Johnny Walker on the rocks, please," Chase said as she sat on the stool.

"Red, black, or blue?" the bartender asked as she waited.

"Blue."

The gray-haired woman nodded and began filling a small glass with ice.

"Do you always get everything the way you want it?" Chase heard the sultry voice in her ear. She slowly turned to face the woman that slid onto the stool next to her. *Oh no.*

"Dr. Centrino, how are you?" she asked nonchalantly. The woman that she almost let seduce her at the last conference in New York had found her in a matter of ten minutes. How was she going to get through this week? And how the hell was she supposed to handle this gorgeous woman throwing herself at her all week?

"Ah, you remember me. I was hoping you hadn't forgotten. I never saw you again in New York. I very much wanted to see you again." Sahara Centrino's eyes were dark with desire, almost as black as her long hair. Her olive complexion contrasted nicely with the sleeveless ivory blouse she was wearing and showed a hint of cleavage since the first two buttons were open. Her tight black skirt stopped just above her knees. The matching jacket that she'd been wearing earlier that day was now lying on the bed in her room.

How could I not remember you? I was practically fucking you on the dance floor! "I attended different meetings, I guess," Chase said as she sipped the golden liquid in her glass, refusing to meet her eyes. The slight burning sensation set her body on fire as the scotch washed down her throat. Her attempts at calming her libido backfired. She found herself physically attracted to the alluring woman next to her.

"Maybe this time we'll find ourselves on the same page." Sahara sipped the Dirty Martini in front of her.

My god this woman breathes sex! Talk about pheromones, holy shit! Chase knew it would be a bad idea going to bed with this woman. She did not need a one-night stand right now, and she definitely didn't need strings. Getting over Remy Sheridan was hard enough as it was. Getting involved with someone else would escalate the situation. Nope, she'd say goodnight to the temptress and go take a cold shower.

***

By Wednesday Chase had managed to elude Sahara for two days. She was succeeding on a third when she saw the ebony-haired woman walk through the doorway. *Crap!* She thought to herself as she saw the woman make a beeline for her. This was the last meeting of the day thankfully. Chase had a headache and now she'd have to contend with this woman.

"Fancy meeting you here, I was sure you were avoiding me like the plague." She smiled playfully.

I am. Chase almost said. "I guess we just have separate agendas." Chase shrugged, thankfully the room had quieted, and the first speaker started.

"Maybe we can go talk when this is over," Sahara whispered as she squeezed Chase's hand then let go.

By the time the seminar on the latest line of arterial stent technology was over, Chase's headache had subsided.

Still, the velvety smooth scent of Sahara's perfume tickled her nose and teased her libido. Chase gathered her notes and closed her briefcase. Sahara grabbed her arm before she could disappear again.

"Walk with me," she said with thirsty eyes. Chase blew out a shaky breath and followed her out of the large room. Once they were out in the hallway a few other women joined them.

"Hi, it's good to see you again." One of the women gave Chase a quick hug. "Why don't we all go to dinner together? I'll round us up a Limo." The auburn-haired woman disappeared. *Great,* Chase thought. Now she was stuck with them for the night. She never really spoke to these women outside of the conferences that she attended.

"I need to go change clothes. I don't want to be in a suit all night." Chase wrinkled her nose.

"Me too!" Sahara followed her into the elevator, the door shut before anyone else could join them. "What room are you in?"

To lie or not to lie. Chase weighed the pros and cons. She could have a night of unruly, lustful sex with this beautiful woman, or she could throw her guard up and put her foot down. Then again, she could quickly change into jeans and go out dancing with the group.

"I'm in 709, but I'm just going to change and come back down. I'll see you in the Limo," Chase said as she pushed number seven.

"You were very different in New York," Sahara said as she pressed number five.

It's now or never. Chase thought as she pressed the stop button on the wall. She wanted to slam Sahara against the back of the elevator and take her in one swift motion. Instead, she settled for reality. "Look, you're a very attractive woman, Sahara, and I don't deny my attraction to you, but I'm not looking for a relationship. I have too much on my plate as it is."

"Chase, I know we can't have a relationship. You live in Miami and I'm in Chicago. I'm attracted to you too; I haven't been with very many women since my husband, and I split up. I haven't come out to anyone back home, so technically I haven't even had a relationship. I guess I'm still in the 'have fun' stage," she sighed. "Do you have a girlfriend waiting for you at home?"

Chase stared at the floor, and then met her eyes. "No. But, it's complicated. I just don't want to spend the night with you and then you expect more from me. I can't have that, not now, not ever." Chase knew she sounded harsh, but she needed to let this woman know where she stood.

"Whoever she is, she hurt you badly. I can see it in your eyes." Sahara put her hand on Chase's cheek. "You're in love with her." Chase closed her eyes. "How about we go to dinner and have a good time tonight. Whatever happens, happens and we take it from there, okay?"

Chase nodded and opened her eyes.

"I'm not going to stop, Dr. Leery. I want you and I want you badly, but I'm willing to let it go this time." She smiled playfully and Chase shook her head.

***

The dance floor was full of sweaty bodies grinding along to the beat of *Paradise by the Dashboard Lights*. Sahara grabbed Chase's hand and pulled her to the dance floor. Both women were smiling and dancing fast together. The group of women they were with drank a few pitchers of

Sangria at dinner and switched to pitchers of beer once they arrived at the *Moon Doggy*. Chase could feel the sweat running down her back, but she was enjoying herself and dancing her ass off with the rest of the crowd of men and women. Sahara playfully wiggled her eyebrows and ran her hands seductively over Chase's chest and up into her hair. She pulled Chase down into a smoldering hot kiss when the woman's voice began the famous exchanging lines of the song. Chase broke the contact first and playfully pushed her away when Meatloaf started his part of the lines. Both women laughed and continued dancing.

"I'm worn out." Chase emptied her glass of beer and poured herself another. "I'm too old for this shit," she laughed.

"I'm older than you, honey!" one of the other women in their group said as she took off to the dance floor with a man that offered his hand. The DJ must have been doing a Meatloaf tribute because he played *Anything for Love* next and Chase felt her entire body shudder. She parked her butt on a stool and proceeded to cry into her beer. Lucky for her it was dark in there and no one saw the tears. *Damn you, Remy Sheridan!* By the time the others made it back from the dance floor her face was dry once again.

Eventually, the long songs ended, and the DJ turned the heat back up with Michael Jackson's *The Way You Make Me Feel*. Sahara grabbed Chase's hand and led her back to the sweltering center of the room. They found that it was impossible to dance to this song unless they were grinding their bodies together. Chase felt her hips slide against Sahara's causing the center of her jeans to dampen. She knew it wouldn't take much, a few more beers and dances like this and she'd be begging for release. Sahara turned around at that moment to rub her ass against Chase's crotch. *My god! I'm dying here!* The woman was good, damn good. Chase couldn't help feeling a sexual attraction, hell any sane woman with a heartbeat and a clit would be begging for this woman if she was doing this to them. Chase heard herself whimper when Sahara spun her around and again rubbed up against her back and ran her hands down the front of Chase's body from her handful of breasts to the quivering muscles of her stomach. Neither of them noticed the song change to *Dirty Diana*, talk about seductive. Chase turned herself back around and pulled Sahara tightly into her arms, their bodies welded together as their lips met and fused. Seconds later, both women pulled apart breathless as the song ended.

"I thought we were going to have to turn the hose on you two," one of the women stated with a laugh when Chase and Sahara sat at the table.

"Oh please," Sahara laughed.

Chase kept quiet and poured herself another beer. *I am turning into Gayle,* she thought. "I don't know about you ladies, but I'm tired and I'm still feeling the jet lag, so six o'clock comes early for me." Most of the table agreed with her as they paid for the tab and called the Limo driver.

Chapter 18

"Welcome home, wanna have lunch? You can tell me all about it," Frankie said.

"Thanks. Actually, that's why I was calling. You won't believe the week I've had," Chase sighed and leaned her head against the back of her desk chair. Her scrubs were sweaty from the four-hour triple bypass that she'd just completed. Her head was heavy and her eyes droopy. She was still on California time and the Florida humidity was already kicking her in the rear.

"Can you get away?"

"No, unfortunately I have about ten minutes to inhale a salad and then I'm back in the O.R. I have two more surgeries today." She unknowingly rubbed her temple with her free hand and closed her eyes. "How about dinner?"

"That'll work. I'll meet you at Kojima around eight. I'm in the mood for Sushi."

"Sounds great, gotta go. I'm being paged." Chase closed her cell phone and picked up the receiver for the phone on her desk.

***

Chase was halfway through her last surgical procedure of the day and wrist deep in blood and human tissue as she sewed the new valve into place on the frail man's heart. Her mind was usually clear when she was working. Surgery had always been her escape from the world, for those four to eight hours, it was like having an out of body experience. Except for this particular moment, Remy Sheridan had slowly poured herself into Chase's mind. The blond blinked her eyes and shook her head blaming the jet lag for her lack of concentration. Thankfully, the operation was going smoothly. She would soon be closing his chest. Then, she would staple him down the middle, and send him back to the world to hopefully live several years longer.

***

Chase walked into Kojima shortly after eight. She was freshly showered and wearing a pair of tan khakis and a black, short-sleeved top. Her short blond hair was in dire need of a cut and stuck out in all directions. She spotted Frankie waving at her from a table in the corner.

"Hey!" Frankie stood up and hugged her. "I'm digging the hair, it's sexy on you." She laughed. Chase rolled her eyes and sat down.

"It's getting cut tomorrow!"

"Suit yourself. So, what's new? How was Cali?" Frankie ordered a bottle of Saki when the waitress came over to the table.

"Boring as hell, typical seminar sessions of various MD's and PhD's talking about the human heart, heart surgery, and the tools and equipment used during heart surgery. Blah, blah, blah. But I did run into some other doctors I know. Do you remember my trip to New York a while back?"

"Yeah."

"Remember the woman I told you about?"

"The doctor from Chicago that you almost slept with?" Frankie said as she poured the Saki into two small cups. Chase drank hers quickly.

"Yep. Anyway, she was there and just as hot and heavy for me. We practically picked up where we left off..."

"No way! You were pining for..."

"I know, listen to my story. Anyway, I explained to her that it was only physical, and I never wanted anything more. We both agreed and went out with a few other doctors and spent the night dancing all over each other."

"Wow." Frankie refilled their cups. "Did you sleep with her?"

"Surprisingly, no. I came very, very close though. It would've been raw sex with nothing else, and I already had that right here with Ronnie. I didn't need another notch in my belt for no reason, so I turned her down."

"I'm impressed. I don't know if I could've said no at that point." Frankie smiled.

"It was hard, nearly impossible. Besides, you're single and probably will be for life, Frankie. When's the last time you went on a date or got laid?" Chase smiled.

"Between you, Ping and Gayle, I have plenty of action going on," she laughed. "Who knows. I'm too busy and wrapped up in work to see Miss Right unless she slapped me across the face. Maybe I'll meet her in the Keys." The conversation was broken up long enough for them to order.

"Did you get the plans together yet?" Chase asked.

"Yeah, everyone can go in exactly two weeks, so I booked us Friday, Saturday and Sunday at the hotel that's not far from Duval Street. I also rented two scooters. You and I can drive the other two around."

"That sounds like fun. I'll make sure I put in for no call from Thursday to Tuesday, otherwise they'll screw up and put me on call."

"Yeah, we're not coming back in the middle of the night so you can save someone's life." Frankie winked. As soon as their array of Sushi hit the table, Frankie smiled and nodded towards someone sitting a few tables back from Chase. On instinct, the blond turned around to see who her friend was acknowledging. Chase felt the thorn twist in her side when she met Remy's eyes. They held one another carefully. Chase felt her own eyes turn stone cold before she turned back around.

"I'm sorry," Frankie said.

"Don't be. I know she lives here too, and I'm bound to run into her." Chase swallowed the lump in her throat and tried to eat.

"Let's talk about something else, shall we?" Frankie sipped her sake. "Ping has some woman at work chasing her around. She's not exactly out around the office so it's starting to annoy her. That's all I've heard about for the past week."

"Hmm... nothing like a co-worker to shove you out of the closet headfirst." She remembered how she was 'outed' during her internship when a nurse wanted to play with her during her break. It was good, until they got caught. Chase shook the thought from her head. It was hard for her to sit there and appear oblivious to the woman sitting fifteen feet away from her. Thankfully, her back was to the brunette who seemed to make her weak in the knees with only her eyes.

"Yeah, that same shit happened to Gayle too. I never got it on with a co-worker, so I didn't have that problem." Frankie smiled.

Their plate of sushi finally disappeared, and they fought for the check. Frankie won out with the promise to let Chase get it next time.

"I'm stuffed."

"Me too, I'm surprised I ate," Chase said as she tossed her napkin on the table.

"Maybe it's a sign." Frankie wiggled her rust-colored eyebrows.

"I doubt it." Chase sighed.

Frankie smiled and gave a slight wave to Remy as they walked past her table. Chase didn't have to look over at her to feel brown eyes boring into her soul. *Don't turn around, Leery, be the bigger person. God, why can't I get over her? I am so in love with her that it hurts to even think about it.* Chase shook her thoughts away and continued to walk right out of the restaurant. She hadn't even noticed Remy sitting with an unfamiliar woman.

***

Chase was about to leave the hospital late Thursday night when there was a knock on her office door. She was still in scrubs and tired from working a hundred and two hours for the week. Thankfully, she would be leaving for Key West in the morning and not looking back until Monday afternoon when she would arrive home from her mini vacation. Too tired to get up and open the door, she called for the person to come in as she finished packing up her briefcase. It wasn't until she heard the door click shut that she looked up to face her caller.

"Remy? What are you doing here?" Chase asked. Her voice was barely audible. She felt as though she was looking into a dream or watching an apparition walk towards her.

"Can we please talk?"

Talk! You ripped my heart out and now you want to fucking talk *to me?* "We have nothing to say to each other. At this point, I think we've said all we can. Now, if you'll excuse me, I'm tired and about to be on my way home." Chase stood and maneuvered around the desk towards Remy who was blocking her path to the door. Remy reached out and grabbed her wrist softly. Chase's skin was on fire from the contact, and she dropped her briefcase unconsciously.

"I left Brian." Remy's eyes searched Chase's for any sign of the passion they shared. But Chase guarded her deep green eyes as if they were the windows to her soul.

"What do you want me to say? Congratulations? Or I'm sorry, what happened? Wait, how about you're about eight months too fucking late?" Chase shook her head. "I asked you to stay away from me, Remy, and I meant it."

"I left him for you. I love you, Chase." Tears fell one by one down her creamy tanned cheeks. Chase pulled her wrist free from the light grip Remy had on it. She fought back the urge to wipe the tears away. Instead, she grabbed her briefcase from the floor.

"I think you need to take some time for yourself." Chase took a deep breath. "Figure out who *you* are, Remy." Chase brushed past her, careful not to touch her as she made her way to the door. She turned back around. "Please stay away from me."

Chase felt the tears sting her eyes before she found her Mercedes in the parking garage. She tossed her briefcase in the passenger seat and drove off without ever looking back. She struggled with her conscience all the way home. Part of her desperately wanted to run back, take Remy into her arms, and never let go. The other part of her wanted to run away and never come back, in hopes that Remy Sheridan forgot she ever existed.

Chapter 19

Frankie knocked loudly. Chase swung the heavy door open and invited her into her condo while she finished her last-minute packing.

"Sorry, I had a rough night." Chase shrugged and grabbed her suitcase. She swept the room with her eyes one last time, trying to think of anything that she may have forgotten.

"Me too, I had an unexpected visitor." Frankie waited for Chase to lock the door.

"Who came over? Is Ping still having problems with that office woman?" Chase asked as they walked towards the elevator.

"Not exactly." Frankie stepped to the back of the elevator when the doors opened. "Remy was at my door at ten o'clock last night."

"What!" Chase turned to face her. "You're kidding?"

Frankie sighed. "Nope, she cried on my couch until midnight."

"I guess you know she came to see me then."

"I do."

They packed Chase's bag into the back of the SUV and headed towards Gayle's house. Ping would be picked up last since she lived the closest to the interstate. Chase was glad to see the steaming cup of Starbuck's waiting for her in the console. She smiled and took a long hot gulp.

"I figured you'd need that. I doubt you slept at all," Frankie said as she pointed the SUV towards the main road.

"How much *do* you know?" Chase stared out the window cradling her coffee with both hands and wishing for a banana. *Why the hell do I always crave banana's when I haven't eaten?* She hadn't eaten since breakfast the day before and was starving.

They arrived at Gayle's house within fifteen minutes. During that short time Frankie had repeated the entire conversation between herself and Remy. Frankie knew Remy left Brian and all the circumstances behind that, including her being thrown out in an almost physical fight. Luckily, she'd already signed a month-by-month lease for an apartment, so she had a place to go. Frankie also knew of her profession of love to Chase.

"Can we keep this quiet for a little while? I need to digest everything you told me before I let Jose' and Cuervo know." A smile tugged at the corner of her mouth. She loved all her friends, but Gayle and Ping were the wild ones of the group. They were quick to jump to conclusions and that's not what she needed right now. Especially after hearing how hard it was for Remy to finally leave her boyfriend. No wonder she was always so quiet and shy, the man had been verbally and sometimes physically abusive towards her for years. Chase was suddenly glad that Remy confided in Frankie. She needed to let it all out to someone and Chase was wearing her heart so tightly on her sleeve that she couldn't see past it breaking every time they were around each other.

"That's fine. It's your dirty laundry. You air it out when you're good and ready." Frankie smiled and patted her best friend's hand. "Come on. Knowing Gayle, she's trying to get rid of some girl she picked up last night and still hasn't packed. I promised Ping we'd be there in half an hour."

***

They were at the start of the seven-mile bridge, Frankie was driving the SUV with Chase in the passenger seat and Gayle and Ping in the backseat. Chase finally let the cat out of the bag about Remy. Skimming around the facts, she told them that Remy had left her boyfriend and was now living in an apartment. But she neglected to tell them the details of her horrid relationship or anything about their love for each other. Ping and Gayle wouldn't know love if it slapped them across the face. It wasn't their fault. They just hadn't met the right women yet. Hell, for that matter Chase hadn't really either. The few times that she *thought* she loved someone it came back to bite her in the ass. And Frankie, she had been in love and hurt deeply when her lover left her to go start a family with a man. They had been together for five years and she had considered them married. She thought they'd have a family together. Now, Frankie watched the women come and go from her friends lives and that alone was enough drama to keep her from running into the arms of her own woman. But Chase, that was a different story. They were best friends and know more about each other's lives than anyone else, including most family members.

"Are we there yet?" Ping sighed and stretched her

tiny frame.

"Give me a break, you two sound like you've never been on a road trip." Frankie shook her head. "We'll get there when we get there. How about that?" She shot a smile towards Chase.

"My Dad used to say that to me," Chase said with a small yawn.

"Speaking of him, how are your parents?" Frankie asked.

"Good, I talked to them the other night. I usually call when I get a postcard from a new city. They were up in Vermont soaking up the remainder of the cold weather."

"Gay marriage capital, well it used to be anyway," Gayle said from the backseat.

"It's more than that," Chase laughed. "There are a lot of little antique things for them to do. Plus, Vermont is home to some of the best snow skiing from what I hear."

"Your parents snow ski?" Ping raised her eyebrows.

Chase laughed. "No, but my Dad wants to try his hand at ice fishing, and they have that there too."

"If I was a millionaire, I wouldn't go ice fishing." Gayle shook her head. Everyone laughed after thinking they wouldn't care to do that either.

"Hey that just reminded me, I have a few offers on your paintings," Frankie said to Chase. "I'll pull them up on my computer later if you want."

"Are they in the ballpark?" Chase asked. She hated being nonchalant about it. Her friends knew she was a millionaire, but Chase didn't flaunt it and she never touched her money. Her will left a little to the arts and the rest to the Heart Institute.

"Yeah, I think you'll be pleased."

"I can't believe you're selling them. I couldn't

imagine having that kind of dough," Gayle said.

"Yes, well I never wanted the damn things to start with and the *dough* is going right back into my account where it should've stayed from the beginning." Chase looked at Frankie. "I do have a few pieces in mind in your gallery that I'd like to fill the empty walls with when we get back."

"Which ones?" Frankie asked as she started looking for their hotel.

"I believe they are called *Heavenly Sunshine* and *Imagination's Beginning*."

Frankie raised an eyebrow. "Those are Remy Sheridan's."

"Yes, I know. Despite everything between us, I still like her work. It sort of calls to me, like she paints what I'm thinking or feeling."

"Aww, aren't you quite the romantic," Ping cooed.

"It has nothing to do with romance, Ping Pong. Its art and art calls to people. That's why they buy it," Frankie stated as she pulled into the hotel parking lot.

***

So far, their trip to Key West had been eventful. They went snorkeling and jet-ski riding until they were too tired to move the first full day they were there. They spent their nights doing the 'Duval Crawl' along the most popular strip of bars and clubs in the Keys. Tonight, they found themselves sitting in a fancy restaurant eating lobster tail and drinking wine.

"I don't know about you girls, but I'm spending tomorrow in a lounge chair by the pool," Ping said as she swallowed the last succulent bite of Florida lobster tail.

"Actually, I'm thinking of going deep sea fishing. I've never done that."

"Would you mind if I joined you, Chase?" Frankie asked.

"Sure." Chase smiled. "Can you fish?"

"I don't know. Can you?" Frankie asked quizzically.

"Never tried," Chase laughed. She was feeling adventurous this week. It had been her idea to go snorkeling and Jet Ski riding. If their excursions were left up to Ping and Gayle, the women would be lying by the pool all day and cruising the lesbian bars at night.

"Hmm…"

"I'm staying here with Ping. You guys are nuts." Gayle shot them both a crazy look and shook her head.

"Suit yourself."

***

There were three other women on the large fishing boat. One had shoulder length blond hair that was in a ponytail pulled through the back of her baseball cap. Frankie had done the same thing with her auburn hair to keep it out of her face all day. The other two women with the blonde had shorter hair, but all three of them were there together.

"Hi, I'm Sonya Walker." The blond stuck her hand out to Frankie as they gathered around waiting for the boat to leave the dock. "This is Janine Stetson," She pointed to the brunette that stood closely to her left side. "And this is Tracey Griffin."

"Hi, I'm Frankie DeLuca and this is Chase Leery." Frankie smiled and shook the soft hand Sonya offered to her. Then, the rest of the women exchanged handshakes.

"Where are you two from?" Janine asked.

"Miami. You?"

"Fort Lauderdale or *Fort Lick her tale* as we like to call it." Sonya smiled.

"I see." Frankie raised her eyebrows and Chase laughed.

The boat took them twenty miles offshore. There the captain and his deckhand set all the women up with poles and bait to get started. They helped the deckhand chum the water and helped cast the lines out into the deep blue ocean.

By noon all the women had caught a fish or two. Chase fought with a large Wahoo that managed to break the line once she got him to the boat, but Frankie was right there to snap pictures of the adventure. After that they stopped to enjoy turkey sandwiches and cold beer for lunch, Chase stretched out on the bow of the offshore cabin cruiser. Frankie went to join her when Sonya asked her how long they had been together. Frankie lost her footing on the slippery deck and Sonya caught her. Frankie let herself stay wrapped in the warm embrace for a minute longer than she normally would have, but something in Sonya's gray eyes made her feel safe. She shook the thought and let it pass.

She laughed softly and smiled as she pulled away to compose herself. "We're best friends, but we're not together. Never have been actually."

"Wow, I thought for sure you two were lovers." Sonya looked surprised. Her sunglasses were sitting on the top of her head, and she felt like covering her eyes to hide her excitement.

"Nope, I've known Chase about seven years. We're probably closer than siblings. As a matter of fact, we are. She's an only child, but we know more about each other than anyone in our families. I guess you could say we're each other's family. We're actually vacationing with two other friends, but they stayed at the pool to sunbathe." She smiled.

"So, none of you are together?"

"No. Just four best friends. I thought you and Janine were together," Frankie said as she sipped her beer.

"No way, she's a drama queen." Sonya rolled her eyes and grinned. "We're all friends too. I'm actually new to the group. I just moved down from Kentucky six months ago for work and they sort of took me in."

"What do you do?"

"I'm a marketing consultant. The pay down here was much better, and it was a promotion with my company, so I transferred. What about you?"

"I own an art gallery."

"Wow, that's interesting. Are you also an artist?"

"God no, but I probably know more about art than the president knows about politics." Frankie grinned.

"Hell, I know more about politics than he does."

"That's true, bad analogy," Frankie laughed and tossed her empty beer can in the trash. Two beers were definitely plenty out in the hot sun on that swaying boat.

"Maybe I'll come see it some time." Sonya winked. "You can give me an art history lesson."

"Anytime." Frankie saw Chase coming back around the cabin towards the back of the boat.

"Let's get back at it, ladies," the captain said as he set up the hooks with fresh bait and the deckhand began chumming the water with bloody fish guts.

Chapter 20

Chase stepped onto the dock and stretched her back. Her hair was windblown and messy, basically in its usual state and her skin appeared a little darker than its natural tan color. She was tired.

"I don't know about you, but I had a hell of a good time. Who knew fishing would be so much fun!" Frankie said as she stumbled trying to regain her shore legs.

Chase grinned. "See and you were worried." She shook her head. "Let's go see what tweedle dee and tweedle dumb got into while we were gone."

"God, do we even want to know?"

"Not really. I could've stayed home and worked on my tan and people watched. Those two crack me up."

"Hold on a sec," Frankie said when she saw the other three women making their way towards a small car. She returned a few minutes later with a large grin smeared across her face.

"Do I dare ask what that was about?" Chase waited for Frankie to hit the locks so she could get into the SUV.

"They're joining us for dinner at Margaritaville at seven."

"I see."

***

Frankie found Chase sitting on the balcony when she went into their adjoining room. She was freshly showered and dressed in lightweight khaki-colored pants and a white tank top. Her flip flops were sitting by the door.

"What's up?" Frankie asked when she sat down next to her in the empty plastic deck chair.

Chase took a deep breath and opened her eyes. She didn't chance a look in her best friend's direction. Instead, she stared out at the setting sun. "Not a whole lot, just tired. Are we leaving?"

"Uh huh, you can't pull the wool over this old broad's eyes. Try again slugger," Frankie teased.

"How did you do it, Frankie? I can't get her out of my head." Chase's voice cracked. "The more I try, the harder it is."

"You're in love with her, honey. It doesn't get any harder than that. Unfortunately, you have to roll with the tide until it flattens."

Chase raised an eyebrow, finally meeting Frankie's eyes. "When did you get so philosophical?"

"I don't know. It just came to me suddenly." Frankie shrugged.

"You have a crush!" Chase jumped at the realization and almost fell out of the chair.

"No, I do not! What the hell are you talking about?"

"Sonya. You like her."

"She's cute and friendly, but I draw the line there."

"Sure you do. Here I am sulking over a relationship that has been doomed from day one and my best friend is doing her damnedest to hide her first real crush in forever. We're a real fucking pair, aren't we?" She laughed.

"Yeah, let's go before Dumb and Dumber walk off. I sent them to the car five minutes ago." She smacked Chase on the arm and stood up. "For what it's worth, Chase, if it's meant to be it'll work itself out."

***

"You two, come on! I'm starving!" Ping yelled at the pair coming down the stairs.

"Hey, I'm not the one that sat in the sun all day and forgot to eat. Don't give me hell for your stupidity! Got it?!" Frankie growled and slid into the front seat of the SUV.

"So, who are the girls? And why are we having dinner with them? Are they hot?" Gayle was barely in the car before the questions started.

Chase mentally wished Frankie would go out without her at least once. She wasn't sure she was in the mood for the entire group tonight.

"Oh god, please tell me they're not fish people," Ping exclaimed.

"First of all, what the hell are 'fish people'? Second, as I told you both, we met them on the boat, and they are a group of friends here on vacation like we are. They are a lot of fun and I guess you could say they're all cute."

"Do you two ever think of anything besides hooking up?" Chase barked.

"Yes, as a matter of fact I'm thinking about food right now." Ping grinned. Chase rolled her eyes and shook her head.

They parked a few blocks away and walked down to

the restaurant. The three women they were meeting were standing on the curb talking and waiting for them to arrive.

"Hey guys," Frankie greeted them. "This is Gayle and Ping, and this is Janine, Tracey, and Sonya. They live in Ft. Lauderdale." All the women shook hands and headed inside to their waiting table. Frankie took the initiative and ordered a couple buckets of beer for the group and Sonya ordered two sample platters.

"So, what do you guys do in Lauderdale?" Ping asked.

"I'm a marketing consultant," Sonya said with a smile directed towards Frankie who was sitting across from her. Chase noticed it and kept it to herself. Frankie deserved to be happy, and this was the first time Chase had seen her this way with anyone. At first the one-night stands came after her break-up, but eventually they ended too.

The conversation continued as Janine talked about working for the postal service for the past eight years and Tracey mentioned she was in real estate. Gayle and Ping went on and on about their jobs and found out the three new women were all in their early thirties.

"So, Chase, I don't remember what it is you do," Tracey said.

"I didn't really talk about it when we were out on the boat." Chase shrugged and finished her beer. "I work at a hospital."

Gayle rolled her eyes and hit Chase's shoulder with her own. "Don't let her fool you. Chase is a heart surgeon at Mount Sinai Hospital and a member of the Heart Institute Board."

"Wow." All three women stopped conversation to stare at Chase. Chase wanted to smack Gayle in the back of her head. She swore she would if Gayle mentioned anything about her money. She felt her ears turning red.

"It's not as glamorous as it sounds, trust me." Chase smiled and ordered another beer.

"I would've never pegged you for a doctor. You look more like a fitness instructor." Janine laughed. The entire table joined her. Ping couldn't help throwing in how physically active Chase was, when she wasn't working.

***

Chase and the gang left the next morning. They exchanged phone numbers and email addresses with the other girls with promises to keep in touch. The ride home seemed twice as long as the ride down. Chase called into her voicemail at the hospital and hung up when she heard the recording say she had twenty-five messages. She wasn't ready to go back into doctor mode. She still had one more day before she needed to come back down to Earth.

Chapter 21

Chase sat at her desk reading the latest medical journal updates while sipping on a cup of coffee. She had just finished a four-hour surgery and she still had two more scheduled before her shift was over. Six weeks had gone by since she'd arrived home from her impromptu vacation. She leaned back in her chair and stretched her spine. She wished she was still rocking with the rolling waves on the offshore fishing boat with a beer in one hand, fishing pole in the other, and nothing on her mind as she watched the tiny fluffy clouds float past the sun in the distance.

She had been at the hospital over eighty hours a week continuously since she returned. Her schedule was a little heavier than normal, but that was a lame excuse. She worked when she was stressed. She worked when she was tired. She worked when she was lost. Lately, she'd been all the above and then some. Working seemed to be the only thing that kept her mind from racing to an adorable brunette with a killer smile and eyes she couldn't say no to. Some people turned to alcohol as a crutch, Chase turned to work. She hadn't necessarily been avoiding her friends, but she was tired of hearing Remy's name come up in conversation.

It wasn't really Frankie's fault. Remy was slowly becoming one of her most sought-after artists. She was already preparing another showing with Remy as the showcase artist in the coming weeks. The rest of her friends were just curious if Chase had been in contact with her since they seemed to run into her from time to time. That was a huge reason why Chase worked and went home. She hadn't been to Rainer's and had stayed away from the local bars since she'd been home. Running into Remy would just be the icing on the proverbial cake and a step she just wasn't ready for.

Chase's pager went off at the same time her desk phone rang. The last thing she wanted to deal with was an emergency call when she had a cardiac patient scheduled for surgery in forty-five minutes. She reluctantly answered the phone and checked her pager at the same time.

"Hey, stranger. You've been avoiding my calls. I figured you'd have no choice but to answer this phone."

"Frankie, I'm not avoiding you. I'm avoiding a situation," she said as she read the message on her pager. "I really have to go. I just got paged to the roof. This can't be good."

"Uh huh, so seriously you can have lunch or dinner with me without 'you know who' coming up in conversation. I'm your best friend for crying out loud, Chase. I know this isn't easy for you."

Chase sighed. "Frankie, really, I have to go. We can talk about this later." She hung up the phone and clipped the pager to her dark blue scrub pants.

***

As soon as the rooftop doors opened Chase was

windblown. The red and white helicopter was sitting in the middle of the pad with the rotors spinning. She assumed this was the emergency she was paged to, so she ducked her head and ran over to the open door. She expected to see an elderly person having a heart attack.

"We have a thirty-three-year-old female stabbing victim," the flight nurse said as he jumped out and began unloading the stretcher.

"Why was I paged? I'm not a general surgeon," she yelled over the loud whooshing sound as the rotors began to slow. This was probably a mistake. She was paged when someone in general surgery or trauma should have been paged. She remembered enough of her ER rotation to be able to assess the situation at least.

"She's been stabbed in the chest and the knife is still in. I believe the blade is possibly lodged in her heart muscle," he said as pulled the stretcher out with the feet end first.

Chase saw the knife handle surrounded by a bloody white sheet and sticking out of the woman's chest. Her stomach dropped and her adrenaline began to race wildly. This was serious, very serious. If that knife really was embedded in her chest, she would more than likely bleed to death as soon as it was removed. No surgeon in the world would be fast enough to save her. Chase had seen some traumatic surgeries during her career, but nothing compared to this moment.

The flight nurse was steadily reading her stats and watching the portable EKG monitor. Her heartbeat was surprisingly stable. Chase wondered if maybe the knife had perhaps missed her heart and arteries all together. It wasn't until they were rushing the stretcher into the hospital that Chase even looked at her face.

Her eyes were closed, and her skin was eerily pale behind the oxygen mask on her face. She appeared almost lifeless, but there was no mistaking the soft features and short brown hair. Chase felt her throat tighten as her own lungs deflated. Remy Sheridan's delicate body was lying on the stretcher racing down the hall to an almost certain death. She felt a tear slip down her cheek. How was she supposed to save this life? Was this some kind of sick joke God decided to play on her? She needed to pull herself together. They would be in an operating room in a few seconds, and she would need to be the award-winning cardiac surgeon Chase Leery, not the woman in love with the patient on the table.

Chase was thankful the flight nurse had the chief of trauma surgery paged to the operating room along with a few of her own staff members to assist. They began taking x-rays as soon as they slid her from the small stretcher to the operating table. Chase quickly changed into her surgical dressing and scrubbed in before she walked into the room.

"It doesn't look good. The knife blade appears to be in the left ventricle and the blade is about two inches long. About three quarters of an inch to possibly an inch of it is embedded. It's your common garden variety pocketknife. At least it's not serrated."

Chase looked at the multiple x-rays. "Is she stable enough to go under?" she asked Dr. Harris Porter, the anesthesiologist, and a colleague that she had worked with hundreds of times. She trusted him.

He took a deep breath. "She's stable. You can see her vitals." He pointed to the beeping and flashing monitors she was connected to. "I can't say what's going to happen when you open her up though. She looks pretty beat up. I honestly don't know if she will remain stable."

At that statement Chase looked at her, really looked at her body and not just the small handle sticking out of her chest. One of her cheeks was bruised and turning purple. When she pulled the sheet back, she saw more bruises starting to form along her abdomen. She slid the sheet back up. Reality finally slapped Chase across the face. This wasn't some accident. Someone beat Remy and apparently tried to kill her. Chase's jaw tightened so hard her she almost broke her own teeth.

"We have no choice. Someone tried to kill this woman and I'm going to do everything I can to save her life." She held her anger in check. She had a job to do. The woman on the table couldn't be Remy Sheridan to her. She had to be another patient that needed her care. Otherwise, she wasn't sure she could keep it together long enough to even attempt the delicate procedure. She slid the scalpel down her chest and watched the thin line of blood run down. She said a silent prayer as a tiny tear fell from her eye.

Chapter 22

Chase was sitting at her desk for the second time that day. She picked up the phone and dialed Frankie. As it rang, her mind drifted back to the three-and-a-half-hour surgery. The knife was actually positioned in a slight angle with most of the blade in the septum, which is basically a thick muscle wall that separates the ventricles. The first few centimeters of the blade punctured the side of the left ventricle. Chase closed the tiny ventricle tear as fast as she could sew. Then, she sewed the septum tear in two layers and closed her chest. Remy would need a small blood transfusion to make up the lost blood, but she was still alive and in a medicated coma to heal her traumatic injuries.

"Hello, stranger. I can't believe you hung up on me earlier, you shit."

"Frankie, you need to get down here as soon as possible. Come straight to my office. If I'm not in here, have the charge nurse page me."

"What's wrong, Chase?"

"Remy is here. I can't get into it on the phone. Just hurry, please."

***

Frankie rushed into the hospital and took the elevator up to the third floor. She had numerous scenarios running through her mind as it raced in all directions. She had never heard fear in Chase's voice, but the painful heavy sound she just heard was the closest she had ever come to it. Remy wasn't the kind of person to cause a scene, so that couldn't be the emergency. She prayed something bad hadn't happened to her. The door was locked when she arrived at Chase's office.

"Can I help you?" a young black nurse asked.

"I'm looking for Dr. Leery. She said to have her paged if she wasn't in her office."

"I'd do it for you, but I'm headed the other direction. Go down the hall and take the first right, you will see the nurse's station. They can call her for you."

"Thanks," Frankie said and turned to go in that direction when she saw Chase emerge from around the same corner. She immediately noticed the hollow look on her face and the way her shoulders were slumped. Something was definitely wrong.

Chase barely made eye contact with her as she walked by and unlocked her office door. Frankie followed her inside and shut the door. She half expected to see Remy inside passed out on the couch.

"Chase, you're scaring me what's wrong? Where's Remy?" she said as she sat in one of the chairs across from the desk.

"She's up in ICU. She was just moved from recovery. She's in a medically induced coma. I'm not sure how long we are going to keep her under. I was just down there assessing her vitals and talking to the chief of intensive care," Chase said as she sat in her swivel chair and wiped a tear that started to form in the corner of her left eye. Damn it, she was stronger than this. She dealt with life and sometimes death every day, but she had never felt this empty. When she finished the surgery, she had gone straight to the chapel and cried until there were no more tears to cry, then she collected herself, put her doctor face back on and went back to work. She wasn't sure she had the energy to do it all over again with Frankie.

"Oh my god, Chase. What happened to her?"

"Someone beat her up pretty good and stabbed her in the chest. The knife stuck into the lower portion of her heart."

Tears fell from Frankie's green eyes. She couldn't form words for a full minute. "Why? Oh my god. Is she going to live?"

"Yeah, it looks like she's going to make it, but she just had major open-heart surgery and her body has been put through the ringer. That's why she's in a coma, so she can heal without putting stress on her heart." She held back the fact that they were watching her vitals constantly. If she went into cardiac arrest, she'd surely die before anything could be done to help her. Chase handed Frankie the tissue box.

"Did you do the surgery?"

"Yes. Remember when I said I was paged to the roof, I wasn't joking. They were bringing her in on the helicopter. I didn't realize it was her until they were pushing her down the hall towards the operating room. Her face was so pale and fragile looking. I honestly thought she would die on the table, Frankie. That was the most agonizing three hours of my life. I had her life in my hands. Hell, I literally held her heart in my hands squeezing to keep her from bleeding to death."

"God, Chase. Why didn't someone else do the surgery?"

"I'm the best, Frankie. That's why *I* was paged. I knew there would come a time when the person on the table would be someone I knew. But that was the hardest surgery I have ever performed. I couldn't let someone else touch her like that and hold her life in their hands. Even if I wasn't paged, I would've surely heard about it and volunteered." Chase put her head in her hands.

"I love her. I love her so damn much and I may not ever get to tell her. How could someone do this to her? Why did I push her away?" There weren't many more tears left to cry, but the few that did drop fell heavily. Frankie ran around the desk and pulled Chase into her arms.

"Remy is a very strong woman, Chase. She knows you care for her. She told me recently that she had never made love to anyone until you. She will pull through this, and you can tell her how you feel if that's what you want to do."

"I'm so damn confused. I didn't believe her. I didn't want the drama. I was tired of the cat and mouse game. I told her to leave me alone. I said I never wanted to see her again. I feel horrible, Frankie. I love her and I treated her like shit and now she's in here struggling for her life. What kind of person does that make me, Frankie? I'm no better than the person that did this to her."

"Oh, Chase, don't say that. You're an amazing person. You're a hell of a doctor. You saved her life! No one would blame you for wanting to get out of that situation. You had every right to tell her to stay away from you. You had no way of knowing this would happen to her. No one did."

"She tried to come and talk to me, Frankie. I didn't want to hear it. What if he did this to her because of me?"

"You're my best friend and I love you to death, but if you really start blaming yourself, I'm going to slap you. Some sick son of a bitch hurt her, not you," Frankie said as she stood up and patted Chase on the shoulder. "Have the cops said anything to you?"

Chase gave her half a smile. "No. But, then again, they don't know I know her. They just questioned me about her injuries right after the surgery and took the knife with them."

"Hopefully, there are fingerprints, and they can catch this bastard."

Chase stood and stretched her back. She needed to splash water on her face for the third or fourth time. "I don't know how to do this. I have to put my doctor's face back on and go check on her. If I let on that I know her or was personally involved with her, I could lose my job for treating her."

"I'm familiar with the policy. I think it's ridiculous. You're the best heart surgeon in the southeast. If something happened to my heart, you could bet your ass I'd want you operating on me. In fact, I think I'm going to call my attorney and have that put in my medical power of attorney and will and whatever else it needs to be in." She smiled.

"Flattery will get you everywhere." Chase grinned. "When this is all over, I am going to need a lot of drinks, very strong ones."

"I think I will too."

"Do you want to go with me to see her?"

"Yes. I need to go to the ladies' room first and wash my face. I don't want to scare anyone."

"I need to go too. I've just about scrubbed the skin

off my face today."

***

Remy was laying slightly elevated on the hospital bed. She had IV lines coming from one arm, an intubation tube in her mouth, and a drain line coming from her chest collecting excess blood. Her pale face was sunken in, she looked much older than the vibrant young woman Frankie knew her to be. She had to turn away to gather herself when she first saw her.

"You can talk to her and hold her hand if you want. She can feel you and hear you. It actually helps, or so they say," Chase said as she went around to the monitors and wrote down her stats on a 3x4 card she kept in her pocket.

"She looks so sad just laying here." Frankie sat on the doctor's stool and took Remy's hand in hers. "I guess I was expecting her to look all beat up."

"Her chest and abdomen are pretty bad. She has a couple fractured ribs, a bruised spleen, and her liver looked a little bruised too in the MRI we did. He didn't touch her face though."

Chase reached down and grabbed her other hand as she leaned towards her face. She kissed her cheek and whispered in her ear. "Remy, it's Chase. I'll be back to check on you later. Frankie is here with you. I love you."

"I'm going to sit with her for a while," Frankie said. "Do you think you can scare me up a cup of coffee?"

"Sure. I was going for one myself." She checked her watch. "I need to go do my rounds. I'll bring your coffee to you first though. Turn your cell phone off, it can interfere with the heart monitor. I'll come back and check on you in a little while."

Chapter 23

Two days later, Chase leaned against the inside of her closed office door. She wiped away the few lonely tears that snaked down her cheek. She had never felt so weak in her life, not even when Yelena had her 'French bitch' claws in her. She needed to pull herself together and very soon before the entire hospital figured out she was moping around over a patient, a patient she was in love with, a patient that didn't deserve to be going through this alone. Over the past month, her mind had wandered back to the night numerous times when she told Remy to stay away from her after she professed her love. If Chase had just accepted the fact that she loves her too and pulled her into her arms like she was aching to do, then none of this would have happened. Remy wouldn't be lying in the bed right now fighting to heal her battered body.

Chase jumped when her pager went off. She saw that it was the ICU number and she quickly called back. There was a chance Remy would wake up at any time since they had been weaning her off the sedative. Three days post-op wasn't too long to be comatose. Hopefully, she would start waking up soon.

"Dr. Leery, there are some officers here asking to see Ms. Sheridan. I told them I needed to contact her doctor since she was sedated."

"You did the right thing. I'll be there in a second." She hung up her desk phone and took a brisk walk down the hall.

When Chase turned the corner, she was met by a very attractive woman in a dark suit. Her long dark wavy hair was pulled up in a ponytail. High cheekbones accentuated her creamy complexion, making her deep blue eyes look like the color of the ocean on a hot summer day. Chase swallowed what little bit of saliva she could muster. *This woman's a cop?*

"Dr. Leery," the woman questioned. "I'm Detective Nikola. I know Ms. Sheridan is still under sedation, but I need to see her anyway. I have some news on her case."

Nikola, ah, I bet she's Greek. No wonder she's beautiful. "What news?"

"I'm sorry I can't disclose." She raised an eyebrow.

"Then I can't let you see her. She's no longer medically sedated, she could wake up at any time and frightening information may cause her to prolong her own mental sedation."

The detective moved away from the nurse's desk and nodded for Chase to follow her. "We know who did this to her. I just need her to wake up and give a statement. I was hoping she might want to wake up."

"What if she doesn't remember anything? Some people who go through a traumatic event lose that particular timing in their memory. If so, making her relive it could be much worse the second time around."

"I'm here to solve a case, Doctor, not get a psychology lesson. The print is a partial and the only way we get him is by her identifying him."

"Excuse me, Dr. Leery." The nurse jumped out of her seat. "The monitors are going wild in Ms. Sheridan's room. I think she may be waking up."

Chase ran down the hall with the detective on her heels. When they reached the third door on the right Chase spun around into her. Beautiful or not, the detective wasn't calling the shots, not in this hospital and definitely not on this patient. "Give her twenty-four hours to completely come around. Her mind has to reboot, and she doesn't need any stress during this process. Leave your card with the nurse and I'll call if she's talking before then."

Detective Nikola gritted her teeth. It was clear she wasn't used to being told no. Chase stood her ground. They were standing as close as lovers, staring each other down as if sizing up the competition. A few of the other nurses in the hall began to stop and watch the display. Finally, the detective backed up a step. "I'll be back in twenty-four hours."

Chase took a deep breath and opened the door. Remy's head turned towards her; big brown eyes rolled around slowly before fixing on their target. Chase smiled in relief when Remy recognized her. The heart monitor began to beep louder, alerting her heart rate had increased.

"Don't try to sit up. You've been through a lot over the past few days and it's going to take you some time to regroup okay," Chase said as she shined the penlight in her eyes and checked the monitors.

When Remy tried to speak, Chase put her finger on dry cracked lips. "Let me get you some water, hold on," she said as she reached for the tray with a pink plastic pitcher full of ice water. She had no idea why they bothered to put those in comatose patients' rooms, it wasn't like they were going to sit up and pour themselves a glass.

Remy took the straw between her lips slowly. After a few sips, Chase pulled the cup away. "Is that better?"

"Yeah," she croaked. "What happened to me?"

Chase wasn't sure what to say, she didn't want to scare her, but she wasn't going to lie to her either. "You had surgery a few days ago and your body has been recovering."

"Everything hurts, I can hardly move," she said slowly.

"It probably will for a few weeks unfortunately." Chase grabbed her hand and squeezed it lightly.

"Are you my doctor?" she asked. When Chase nodded, she reached up to feel her chest.

"What are you doing? Be careful you have IV lines and drain tubes in you." Chase stopped her hand from reaching her chest where a bandage covered the stitch line that ran between her breasts. "Give yourself some time to wake up, Remy. We can talk about everything in a little bit okay." She grabbed Remy's hand and brought it to her face. She turned to hide the tears in her eyes when Remy's warm palm caressed her cheek.

"Chase," Remy breathed her name.

"Hmm." Chase kept her eyes closed and her face towards the floor.

"You look sad." She tried to pick her chin up to see her green eyes, but Chase stood instead.

"I'll send the nurse in to take some new vitals and check your dressing." She looked at her watch. "I've got rounds but I'll be back later. I know it sounds cliché since you just woke up but try to get some rest. I'll see you soon."

***

Chase called Frankie to give her the good news. She wanted to run up and down the halls screaming because she was finally awake and seemed to be recovering just fine. Chase was so damn happy and sad at the same time. She wanted to pull Remy into her arms and kiss her. Instead, she had to play doctor/patient, at least for the time being. Now that she was awake, she'd be going home in a few days and Chase could have the conversation that was eating her away.

Two cups of coffee, rounds, and a short meeting to update the changing ICU staff on Remy's condition and she was heading back into her room. Chase noticed Remy was sleeping when she walked in, so she quietly shut the door and sat on the stool next to her bed. She looked more peaceful than when she was sedated, which had made her appear lifeless with zero movement and shallow breathing. At the moment, Remy's face was fluttering, and she was breathing deeply, two signs of dream sleep instead of dead sleep.

Chase smiled when brown eyes met hers. "Hey there, I said I'd be back." She helped her drink some water.

"I feel like an alligator in the desert," Remy said as she tried to get comfortable, or as comfortable as she could get lying in that bed. She pushed the button to elevate her head and the movement stretched her chest causing her to wince in pain.

"Are you hurting?" Chase rushed to her side.

"My chest hurts. Hell, my whole torso hurts like someone beat me with a hammer." She readjusted her position and finally just settled on being uncomfortable. "The other doctor that came in said I need to get up and try walking. I think he's crazy."

Chase laughed. "He's right. The more you move around, the sooner you will get out of here." She watched as Remy absently rubbed at the dressing covering the staples in her chest.

"My chest itches and hurts like hell," she sighed and settled further into the pillows.

"Remy do you remember what happened to you?" Chase grabbed her hand, loving the way if felt just to hold some part of her when all she really wanted to do was crawl into that bed and hold her until the pain was gone.

"No. You said I had surgery. Was I in an accident?" Her brows creased, she tried to conjure up some kind of memory, but there was nothing there.

"On Tuesday you were attacked by someone in your apartment." Chase watched the color drain from her face. "Whoever attacked you, beat you up badly. You have some internal bruising which is part of the reason your body is so sore. He also stabbed you in the chest."

Remy raised tear filled eyes to Chase and reached up to run her hand over the bandages on her chest. "How bad is it?" she asked as the tears fell in long streaks.

Chase swallowed the lump in her throat and squeezed her hand. "It… you… uh." Chase cleared her suddenly scratchy throat. "You are going to be just fine. There was no damage." Chase forced a smile and stood up. "You need to follow Dr. Toby's orders and get out of this bed." She reached over and wiped away the tears. "Frankie should be here soon. I talked to her earlier. I'll see you again before you get out. You're in good hands." Chase winked and let go of her hand. All she wanted to do was kiss her and tell her how much she loved her, but damn it she couldn't do anything but walk away. If word got out that she was involved with a patient, she could lose her license.

"Chase..." Remy whispered.

***

Frankie watched Remy sleep. The frown lines were slowly disappearing. The nurse gave her two shots into her IV line, she didn't bother to ask what it was, but it knocked Remy out within a matter of minutes. She needed the rest; her body was still recovering. Frankie wondered if Chase should have even told her the story. It couldn't be good for her to be so upset. Frankie had her doubts about those two the instant she saw their little make out session on the security camera in her office. Now, it was as plain as the off-white paint on the walls in the stale room. Those two women loved each other with everything they had. She wasn't sure love was capable of being so deep. She wondered if she'd ever loved like that. No, she was sure very few people in the world ever knew what it was like to meet your soul mate and feel the true push and pull of yin and yang.

Chapter 24

Frankie heard the sobs before she saw the tears. Remy's room was dimly lit with the multi-colored lights from the machines casting a soft glow. She had talked to Chase before going up to the ICU and knew Chase was caught between a rock and a hard place. She'd never seen her friend so empty. Her heart broke for both of them.

"Hey there," Frankie grabbed Remy's hand and sat in the chair on the opposite side of the bed from the monitors and stool Chase had sat on.

"I was attacked." Remy wiped her tears away and cringed from the pain in her chest. She was overdue for her meds, but she was too upset to take them an hour ago when the nurse brought them and now, she was definitely in pain.

"I know, sweetie." Frankie handed her a tissue from the box on the table. "I'm so sorry."

"She acted like it was nothing, like this is routine for her. Well, it's not routine for me, Frankie. How can she sit there in 'doctor mode?' Does she hate me that much?" She sobbed and tears covered her cheeks once again. Her chest hurt so badly and only part of it was from the surgery. She suspected her heart was breaking all over again.

Frankie rubbed her free hand over Remy's as she held it. "Oh, honey, she does care. She has been at your side since the helicopter arrived on the roof with you in it. She saved your life you know."

Remy raised an eyebrow. What had Frankie just said? The pounding in her head was beginning to match the throbbing in her chest. "What are you saying?"

"Remy, I'm not sure how much she told you or…"

"She just said I was attacked, and he stabbed me, but I'm fine. Is she lying? Frankie, tell me… please." she pleaded.

"You are fine… now. Remy," She chewed her bottom lip, something she did when she was nervous. "Are you sure you want to hear this now? Maybe you should rest."

"Damn it! I'm sick of everyone saying I need to rest. I'm stuck in this bed. All I can do is rest for crying out loud. I want to know the truth."

"Chase told you the truth. She just left out a few details." Frankie handed her another tissue. "Chase was on the phone with me when she was paged to the roof to meet the helicopter. She had no idea it was you until you were on your way to the operating room. She said the knife pierced your heart a little bit. She would have to explain that to you. Anyway, she saved your life, Remy." Frankie watched the tears fall again. "And she has been at your side every hour checking on you until you woke up."

"Then why is she so cold? She runs out as soon as she comes in. She barely talks to me." She cried. "I love her so damn much and I don't know how else to tell her, Frankie. She doesn't want me back."

"Remy, she's a doctor, a very highly respected doctor at this hospital and in her field. If she let on that on that she has feelings for you or has ever been involved with you, she could get into serious trouble. She could lose her license. Doctors aren't supposed to treat patients they know, it's against the law, sweetie. You have no idea how hard it is for her to see you like this and not be able to take the pain away. The woman hasn't slept in days, hell, probably months. I don't think I have ever seen her so sad in all the years I've known her. Remy, she loves you, she's just not able to show it, not here, not like this."

Remy just stared at her. She didn't realize Chase risked her career to save her life. Here she was being selfish because Chase was acting like a doctor, when that's what she was first and foremost, a doctor. She wished she could see her but knew that wouldn't happen anytime soon. "I... Frankie, can you get the nurse."

Frankie jumped up. "Is everything okay? I knew I shouldn't have said anything."

"It's alright." Remy squeezed her hand. "I'm just in a lot of pain. I need my meds." She sighed and laid her head back on the pillow. Thin lines ran across the center of her forehead in tiny creases. She was obviously in serious pain and had been fighting against it.

Chapter 25

Chase poured a few ounces of bourbon into a rocks glass and leaned with her back against the kitchen counter. This was her first glass, and she was looking forward to the slow descent into the land of numbness. She had just finished an all-night shift at the hospital; the sun was peaking over the horizon.

It had been three long weeks since the afternoon she got the page to the roof of the hospital where Remy's life hung in the balance. She'd walked out of the hospital two days ago with barely a sign that she'd almost died, except for the pale deathly look that all the patients seemed to have. She'd smiled at Chase when she walked past her in the hallway, a courtesy smile for the doctor that saved her life. Only Chase saw the pain swirling in the depths of her brown eyes.

Chase swallowed the golden liquid and set the glass in the sink. She snatched her keys off the counter, not bothering to shower the night away or change out of her scrubs. She put the top down on her convertible Mercedes and headed in the one direction that seemed to make it hurt less.

***

Remy's apartment was closer to the hospital than Chase's beachfront condo. Chase wondered if the dark stain on the staircase was Remy's blood as she stepped over it. She wondered why she hadn't taken Frankie up on her offer to stay with her while she recovered.

Chase knocked softly on the crème-colored door to apartment four-twelve. She ran a hand through her hair and waited. *Remy is probably asleep*, she thought as she checked her watch. The sun had just risen, and it was barely six o'clock. She started to step away when she heard the lock click.

"Chase," Remy whispered with a raspy voice, she'd obviously been sleeping. She pulled the door open enough to allow Chase to enter. She was dressed in a loose baby blue t-shirt that rose just enough to show the bottom of her black panties. Her short brown hair was sticking out in all directions. She was adorable, sexier than ever. Chase felt her chest ache and her stomach flip flop. God, she missed her.

"I'm sorry I woke you. I just... I had to see you." Chase sat on the couch next to Remy and reached for her hand. "I'm sorry about a lot of things."

"I understand. I don't want you to lose your job for saving my life, Chase."

Chase raised an eyebrow.

"Frankie explained everything. I just wish you would've told me. I thought you truly did hate me." Remy bit the inside of her lower lip, a gesture Chase recognized as nervousness.

"I don't hate you, Remy. I could never hate you. I

was so scared someone would see me crying at your bedside night after night and moping around like I was lost. When you woke up, I knew you would be okay. I had to pull away. I'll never do that again. I'd rather lose my career than watch you suffer in pain and not be able to hold you in my arms and kiss away your tears." Chase squeezed her hand and slid closer to her. "I'm sorry for so many things, Remy. First, for pushing you away. I keep asking myself if this would've happened to you if I hadn't told you to go away and leave me alone. I…"

"It would've happened anyway." Remy stared at the floor. "The detective was here yesterday. I had to ID my attacker." She took a deep breath, surprised to see the pain in her chest had subsided since she'd been home and sleeping in her own comfortable bed. "Chase, the partial print on the knife belonged to Brian."

"Oh god." Chase pulled her close and wrapped her arm around her. "I had a feeling, but I didn't want to believe it."

Remy had spent all day yesterday crying over what happened to her and finding out who was to blame. She felt safe in Chase's arms, alive. "He's going away for a very long time. Knowing that is helping me move on."

Chase pulled her into a tight embrace, then backed away enough to look into her chocolate eyes. "I…"

Remy put her hand on Chase's cheek and looked into her green eyes. "Please stop saying you're sorry." She smiled. "I kind of want to put everything behind me. I feel like I've been given a second chance and I'm not going to dwell on what may or may not have happened and what if."

Chase smiled. "I like the sound of that. Maybe I should take your advice. Maybe my life wouldn't be so damn complicated." She closed the small distance between them and pressed her lips to Remy's softly. "How are you feeling by the way?"

"Much better now." Remy grinned and pulled Chase to her for another kiss, this one much more intense.

When Remy's tongue stroked hers, Chase's body burned a slow burn from head to toe. She wanted this woman. She was the gasoline and Chase's body was the match. No matter how hard these two tried they couldn't control the fire that burned between them melting everything in its path. It had been that way since the day they laid eyes on each other. Chase followed Remy's lead when she leaned back on the couch. She kissed Remy like she was the oxygen her body craved, deeply and passionately stroking her tongue, her lips, running her mouth down her jaw, across her neck in light kisses and back to her lips for another searing kiss.

Remy moaned softly and thrust her hips up to meet Chase's body hovering above her. Chase ran her hand down the front of Remy's soft t-shirt and onto the soft skin of her taut belly to the top of her panties. She needed this woman like a fish needed water. She ran her hand over the outside of her panties to cup her. Remy thrust her hips again to meet the hand against her. She was soaking wet and throbbing, she craved Chase's touch.

"Please…" she whispered. "I'm so close."

"You just had major surgery, on your heart of all things. Maybe we should wait."

Chase saw the desire burning in her eyes and in one swift motion pulled her panties down, ran her fingers through the wet folds and entered her softly. Remy moaned and tangled her fingers in Chase's short blond hair. She matched her thrust for thrust as she pulled the back of her scrub shirt up so she could run her hands over the warm flesh on Chase's back covering the subtle defining muscles of her toned body.

"You feel so good," Chase whispered in her ear as she ran her mouth along her jaw biting softly.

Remy's body was climbing the walls she was so close. It had been so long, too long. She felt herself tighten around Chase's fingers. "Make me come, Chase..."

Chase used her free hand to pull Remy's t-shirt up over her small round breasts. She alternated licking and sucking harder as she pushed her fingers as deep as they would go over and over. She was soaking wet and hard just from touching Remy. She knew it wouldn't take much to send her over the edge. "Touch me," she said as she pushed Remy's hand inside her scrub pants.

As soon as Remy ran her fingers around her clit she tightened and jerked. Both women were panting and thrusting against each other as they came together. Chase moved to the side slightly to keep her weight off Remy's chest. She was still taking deep breaths as her body slowly came back down from the euphoric high. She leaned down and kissed Remy softly.

"I should have said this a long time ago. I love you, Remy."

Remy wrapped her arms tightly around Chase and pulled her down for another kiss. She lingered for a second letting her lips rub against Chase's. "I love you too, Chase. I think I've loved you since the first time you kissed me."

Chase pulled back and climbed off the couch. She reached for Remy's hand and pulled her up off the couch.

"What's wrong?" Remy asked, her arms going around Chase's waist.

"I'm assuming you have a bed here somewhere right." She grinned.

Remy laughed. "Down the hall, tiger." She pulled Chase against her for another kiss, this time sucking her tongue and biting her lip softly before ending the kiss. They walked down the hall with their arms wrapped around each other. Remy pushed Chase against the wall just outside of the open doorway and slid her hand into her scrub pants again. She smiled when her fingers found the wet folds they were searching for and slid inside her easily. Yes, she was definitely much, much better.

About the Author

Graysen Morgen was born and raised in North Florida with winding rivers and waterways at her back door and the white sandy beach a mile away. She has spent most of her lifetime in the sun and on the water. She enjoys reading, writing, fishing, and spending as much time as possible with her partner and their children.

You can contact her and like her fan page on Instagram @graysenmorgen

www.tri-pub.com

Made in United States
Troutdale, OR
03/03/2025